Snowflake Sugar

Janet Koops

BROWN HOUSE BOOKS

Book Cover by: The Cover Collection

1st edition 2024 by: Brown House Books

ISBN (print): 978-1-963745-00-9

ISBN (ebook): 979-8-9865521-9-4

Also By Janet Koops

Romance

Magic in Mistletoe
Snowflake Sugar

Women's Fiction

Homing Instinct
Six Weeks With You
Rules of Disengagement
Family Friends
Then I Met You

For a complete list of titles and where to find them,
please visit janetkoops.com.

Chapter 1

As Rosie Plum stood amidst the quiet candy shop, a twinge of uncertainty crept into her heart. A question lingered, as delicate as the sugar strands she twirled—had she made the right choice by becoming co-owner of the candy store?

Not that she didn't like the store. Quite the opposite. She loved every day she worked at the Snowflake Sugar Shop. It was a dream come true when Mable hired her four years ago. Since then, Rosie had poured her heart into creating confectionery art, her hands dancing with sugar and chocolate, weaving sweet dreams for the small town's residents. But the shop at that time, much like the quaint town itself, survived on the whispers of tradition and the support of the occasional tourist. So when Mable passed away, Rosie's world in Mistletoe, Alaska, had turned as fragile as the spun sugar she sculpted.

And then, Sadie, Mabel's granddaughter, arrived like a winter storm, bringing with her winds of change that Rosie could never have anticipated, not only for the store but the entire town. Thanks to Sadie's initiative, Mistletoe transformed from a sleepy town into a year-round Christmas village, attracting tourists like moths to a flame. And in the heart of this transformation came an offer Rosie couldn't refuse—to become a co-owner of the shop she adored.

Now she wondered if she made the right decision.

As a talented confectioner, Rosie took immense pride in her work. Her parents had owned their own business and instilled in Rosie a strong work ethic. And Rosie carried that with her every day. But unlike her parents, Rosie never dreamed of owning her own business. She simply wanted to make candy. That's what got her out of bed in the morning. That's what motivated her best creations. Deep down, she knew that investing in the shop was the right decision, but it came at the price of increased stress and worry.

And now, with Sadie away on her honeymoon, Rosie had full responsibility for the candy shop. The upcoming Valentine's season meant everything to her, not only because of the potential profits but also as a personal testament to her ability to successfully manage the store.

She swept her curly red hair back into a ponytail and grabbed her sketch pad from underneath the counter. "Alright, Rosie. Let's do this," she murmured, tapping her pencil against the clipboard in her hand.

Valentine's Day was four weeks away and bound to be busy, especially those last few days leading up to the fourteenth. Things had quietened down in January as few tourists wanted to celebrate Christmas right after December, so sales had slumped, and the store needed Valentine's Day to turn things around. "I need something attention-grabbing to make a splash on social media," she said to the empty store and opened her sketch pad, flipping the pages until she found the blown sugar heart-shaped bowl. While far from captivating, it was an excellent project with which to warm up her sugar-blowing skills before taking on a larger project.

Clad in her favorite apron, Rosie's face was a picture of concentration as she carefully heated the sugar, her cheeks flushed from the effort and the warmth of the kitchen.

The sugar softened under the heat, turning into a viscous, glowing, red, pliable ball. With years of experience, Rosie knew the right moment to blow. She put the tube to her lips and began to shape the molten sugar, her breath steady and controlled.

However, despite her expertise, Rosie was facing an unexpected challenge. Instead of forming into the smooth, symmetrical shape of a traditional heart, symbolizing love and affection, the sugar had a mind of its own. Each attempt resulted in a messy creation that looked more like a human heart than a Valentine's one. Too bad it wasn't Halloween.

Frustrated but determined, Rosie wiped the sweat from her brow and prepared for another attempt. The sugar glowed under the light, ready to be molded by her skilled hands. She shook her arms and stretched her fingers, hoping her vision would come to life this time. But again, she failed.

"I don't understand," she muttered, pouring herself a coffee. She walked over to the storefront window as the late Alaskan dawn broke, making the snow glisten under the cold sun like a million tiny crystals. The store didn't open for another hour. She could take a walk or, better yet, lie in the snow and make a snow angel. As a child, her mother always had to call her in: "Rosie, come inside before you freeze to death." But Rosie never felt the cold and always lived somewhere with a snowy winter. Why people complained, she never understood. Yes, on occasion, it caused mayhem. So did any extreme weather. But overall, snow was invigorating and beautiful. Each snowflake was unique, yet part of a great tapestry, where every detail, from the intricate patterns of frost on a windowpane to the gentle curve of a snowdrift, was an expression of snow's quiet yet fleeting beauty. Maybe that could be the inspiration she needed for her Valentine's Day project.

So lost in thought, the pounding on the back door nearly gave her a heart attack. Of course. Her delivery was right on time.

Wiping her hands on her apron, adorned with tiny, embroidered lollipops, she hurried to greet the delivery man.

"Morning, Rosie," called Jim, the regular delivery guy, with a grin. "Got a big order for you today."

His emphasis on 'big' puzzled her. She didn't recall this order being any different from her usual one, except for a few more boxes of Isomalt. Her eyes widened in disbelief as Jim unloaded box after box.

"Jim, this seems like more than ten pounds of Isomalt."

Jim checked his clipboard, his brow furrowing. "According to this, it's a hundred pounds. Must be quite the project."

Rosie's stomach knotted. "A hundred pounds? There must be some mistake."

"Don't think so," Jim said. He pulled up her order on his phone. "Here it is. You even signed off on it being a special order."

She chuckled nervously, staring at the screen. "What does that mean?"

"It means I can't take it back."

"But Jim..."

"Think of it this way," he said, navigating the dolly stacked with boxes into the store. "You won't have to buy any more for months and months."

As they stacked the boxes, Rosie began laughing nervously. "This is ridiculous. Look at how many boxes there are."

"I think it's time to experiment," he said, wiping his brow.

Rosie stood amidst the towers of Isomalt. "I wanted to work on my sugar art, but not in this volume."

"Well, if anyone can figure out what to do with all of this, you can, Rosie."

"Thanks," she said, her optimism draining out of her like water from a leaky sink.

Rosie didn't have time to dwell because it was time to open the store, and she spotted a woman waiting out front. Perhaps they'd have a good sales day. "Good morning, and welcome to the Snowflake Sugar Shop," Rosie said, holding the door open. The middle-aged woman nodded and smiled, then began perusing the rows of candy before shaking her head and sighing.

"Is there something special you're looking for, ma'am?" Rosie asked.

The woman looked up from the red velvet box full of truffles in her hand. "I'm not quite sure yet," she said. "I'm here on business and flying home later today. It's my anniversary, and my husband has a huge sweet tooth, but it's hard to find something at this time of year that is not left over from Christmas or set up for Valentine's Day." She pulled out her phone, giving it a quick glance. "I'm also pressed for time."

"Well, you've come to the right place," Rosie said. "Let me think for a minute." She closed her eyes and thought of all the confections she'd been working on. An idea popped into her head. "I've got it. I have something in the back I think you might like." Rosie left, then returned with a small tray. "These are some new things I've been working on. They're called stained glass snowflakes. Made entirely of colored sugar, they are certain to satisfy any sweet tooth."

"They're quite stunning," the woman said, staring at the snowflakes in various colors.

"What if we lay them in a box and then put two of our love bird truffles on top? The truffles nest together, forming a heart and have an ice wine filling."

"That sounds lovely," the woman said, wiping a tear off her cheek. "Oh my, I'm sorry. But this has flooded me with emotion. On the day we were married, it was snowing large beautiful snowflakes. You reminded me how lucky I am that after ten years, I am still madly in love with my husband, and he is with me."

"That's wonderful," Rosie said, trying to ignore the twinge in her heart. She'd yet to meet any-one who filled her with the kind of love this woman had for her husband. Not that she'd been looking. Her life was quite full the way it was. But sometimes, she wondered what it would be like, especially after working with Sadie during her blossoming relationship with Martin Kringle. Rosie shook her head, clearing her mind. Now was not the time. She focused on packaging the candy and handed a beauti-fully wrapped box to the woman. "That will be thirty-five dollars, please."

"It's worth every penny," the woman said, pay-ing for her purchase. "Thank you so much. With candy like this, I imagine you will be overrun come Valentine's Day."

Rosie smiled. "I never complain about being busy. And I'll have help." Nora, Martin's daugh-ter, worked there part-time. Then there was Jack Kringle, a cousin of Martin's who was ap-parently filling in for Sadie. He'd yet to arrive, so she wasn't holding her breath.

As the day wore on, Rosie attended to a small but steady stream of customers, offering sam-ples of her latest confections and suggesting personalized gift ideas for their loved ones. In between transactions, she couldn't help but steal glances at the clock, silently calculating whether they were on track to meet their sales goals. And oh, how that order mistake would hurt their bottom line. She'd need to figure out a solution before Sadie returned. It's not that she'd never considered the store's sales before, but that had never been her primary concern. Now she had to wear two hats, one for business owner Rosie and one for confectioner Rosie.

Could she do both? Fear of failure followed her around like a shadow. She loved her friends and all the quirky characters in their crazy Christmas-themed town. Not to mention the store. What would happen if she let them all down?

Chapter 2

J ACK KRINGLE DESCENDED THE bus steps with effortless grace, his stylishly tailored coat billowing behind him. The air was crisp and cool as he inhaled the fresh mountain air, clearing his lungs of the hot, dry, and stale bus air. "Welcome to Mistletoe: Where the Holiday Spirit Never Ends," a sign cheerfully greeted him. He gave a small chuckle. Just what he needed. A town that celebrated Christmas all year. As if being part of the Kringle family wasn't enough.

While he'd previously visited his cousin, Martin, he'd gone directly to Martin's cabin outside of town. Now he glanced around at the picturesque village, with its decorated town square and enormous Christmas tree, feeling both charmed and slightly out of place.

He saw a sign for the Snowflake Sugar Shop and headed in that direction. "Better late than never," Jack muttered, picking up his duffle bag and adjusting the leather satchel slung across his chest. He'd arrived two days late, but he hadn't been able to resist making a few stops along the way, enjoying the sights and sounds of his journey from Switzerland. His chocolatier training had been intense, so certainly, he could relax for a few days before starting at the Snowflake Sugar Shop. Besides, it wasn't like he signed a contract or anything. This was simply a favor for Martin and Sadie.

Jack took in the vibrant colors and festive decorations adorning each building as he made his way through the quaint town square. He couldn't help but smile at seeing children laughing and playing in the snow. How odd it must be for them to be surrounded by Christmas decorations all year round. Wouldn't that diminish the specialness of the season? It didn't for his family, but to call his family unique was an understatement.

Jack approached a store with a sign above the sidewalk of a magnificent white snowflake against a pale blue backdrop, creating an illusion as if it were delicately crafted from sugar. "This must be the place," he said, and indeed it was. 'Snowflake Sugar Shop' was etched in glass on the store's door. The storefront was nicer than he expected for such a small town. The old building had undergone a meticulous restoration, reverently bringing back to life its early twentieth-century charm. Large, inviting display windows lined the approach, showcasing a mesmerizing array of sweets and treats, each meticulously arranged as if for a glossy magazine shoot. On the ground lay elaborate, patterned tiling leading the customer to a large wooden door, replete with a large glass pane and adorned with ornate brass hardware, gleaming under the store's welcoming lights. It hit him that working there might not be so bad after all. Perhaps Sadie's business partner found the same joy and satisfaction in this sweet endeavor as Jack found in his passion for working with chocolate.

The scent of sugar and warm spices enveloped Jack the moment he stepped into the store. He closed his eyes, inhaling deeply, connecting to the world of sweets surrounding him. Confection was no passing interest to Jack, unlike so many other careers he'd tried. Being a chocolatier was the first thing he had ever truly committed to in his life. Known for losing interest in things quickly, his enduring love of chocolate surprised his entire family, himself included.

The transformation from simple cocoa beans into a myriad of irresistible confections was akin to magic—something his family knew about, so that was saying something.

"Excuse me, are you Jack Kringle?" A voice disrupted his reverie.

Jack opened his eyes and faced the most stunning woman, with vibrant, curly red hair cascading around her face like a ruby water-fall. Delicate freckles adorned her nose and cheeks, and the gentle lines etched at the corners of her mouth revealed a history of abundant laughter. But she was not smiling now. Her striking green eyes, which had the potential to sparkle like an emerald in the sun, glared at him with the power of Medusa.

Jack swallowed. "Ah, yes. That's me." He offered a charming smile, attempting to downplay the tension. "Apologies for my tardiness. I got a bit...sidetracked on the way."

"Well, you're here, so never mind that now. I'm Rosalind Plum, but everyone calls me Rosie."

"Martin has told me so much about you," Jack said, extending his hand for a friendly shake. "It's a pleasure to meet you, Rosie."

"Likewise," she replied curtly, returning the handshake firmly. "Would you like a tour, or is there somewhere else you need to be?"

He noticed her eyeing the duffle bag over his shoulder. "Oh, no. It's fine. I'll drop my stuff off at Martin's later. I'm eager to see the shop and the kitchen facilities."

"We're a small store in a small town, Jack. I'm sure we can't compare to where you worked in Switzerland." Her tone hit as icy as the streets outside.

Martin had described Rosie as fun, outgoing, and optimistic. This woman was tense, curt, and on edge. "It has more to do with the quality of the chocolate and the vision and skill of the chocolatier than the state of the kitchen, wouldn't you agree?"

"So if you're so good, hot shot, why did you have the time to come to Mistletoe and help out little old me?"

"What? No. You've taken that the wrong way. All I meant is that there is no direct correlation between top-of-the-line tools and excellent products. Of course, you need good quality chocolate, but once you have that, it's about passion, vision, and creativity."

"I know what you mean. I feel that way about sugar work," Rosie said, and Jack noted how her eyes lit up. "There's nothing like crafting something beautiful and unexpected. It's chemistry, but there is definitely an art to it, a blend of skill and imagination. And oh, the joy of witnessing someone savor one of our creations is incomparable—watching their expression shift from curiosity to bliss. That is when the true reward of our craft is realized. Each candy is not merely a treat, but an experience, a cherished memory in the making."

"Yes, exactly," Jack agreed.

"Alright then," Rosie said, clapping her hands and shattering the shared moment. "Let's get on with it."

Jack nodded, hit with a surge of enthusiasm at the prospect of sharing his passion with another. He'd previously believed the store sold mostly prepackaged items, despite Martin's attempts to have him check out their Instagram page—something he would undoubtedly do later that night. If Rosie allowed him to experiment, he could stir things up and give this town something completely unexpected.

Perhaps a month in Mistletoe wouldn't be so bad after all.

Chapter 3

J ACK ALWAYS ENJOYED STAYING at Martin's cabin. The guest room was spacious, and the company was entertaining. On this trip, Nora, Martin's teenage daughter, and Ellie, Martin's personal assistant, welcomed him with open arms. They had prepared his favorite dinner and spent the evening listening to stories from Jack's time in Switzerland.

"Don't you miss family?" Nora had asked after Jack reminded them that he'd be on his way as soon as Sadie returned.

"Of course, but I enjoy traveling, and I feel sound knowing that wherever I go, I can always visit family if necessary. That's the beauty of having our folk all over the world," he'd told her. What he didn't admit was that having a family as large and as important as the Kringles could be suffocating—especially if you were different.

The following morning, Jack arose early feeling refreshed and ready to start work. He hadn't made the best impression on Rosie—not that she'd been particularly charming either—but he wanted his time there to be pleasant, so he vowed to make a better impression.

He arrived at the Snowflake Sugar Shop to find Rosie hard at work boxing candy.

"What can I do?" Jack asked, determined to prove himself.

"I need to get these online orders done so they can make this morning's mail pickup. You can start by washing the dishes. When those are done, you can help me wrap candy."

"You want me to do the dishes?" Jack couldn't hide the shock in his voice. He didn't study in Switzerland to wash dishes.

"I don't know what it was like where you were before, but here we do whatever is required. Consider yourself a Jack of all trades."

"Hilarious."

"I'm not joking, and I suggest you put on an apron so you don't get that cashmere sweater all wet and dirty."

Jack gritted his teeth. Martin was going to owe him big time for this.

He spent the next thirty minutes washing dishes, then cleaned the kitchen from top to bottom. There was no way Rosie would find fault with his work. But the thought of him doing this for the next month was unappealing. He feared he might not be a good fit, causing him to move on sooner rather than later.

Just as that last thought crossed his mind, the door chime rang, signaling a customer's arrival.

An older woman entered, browsing the display case with uncertainty. Jack seized the opportunity, drying his hands and moving to the front of the store before Rosie could stop him.

"Good morning, ma'am," he greeted her warmly, stepping around the counter. "My name is Jack. Is there anything in particular you're looking for?"

"Actually, yes," the woman said, her eyes scanning the array of treats. "My granddaughter's sixteenth birthday is tomorrow, and she loves chocolate. I thought I'd surprise her with something special."

"May I make a suggestion?" Jack asked.

The woman nodded.

"Excellent," he said and directed her over to the truffles. "Our truffles are truly exceptional. They're made with the finest chocolate and handcrafted to perfection. We have a variety of flavors, so your granddaughter can enjoy a delightful assortment. Not only that, but truffles also represent a sophisticated chocolate that moves one from the world of childhood candy into one of complex flavors. This will show your granddaughter that she is now viewed as an adult and, as such, deserves a taste of luxury."

"Oh, my," the woman's face brightened, clearly intrigued. "Well, that does sound lovely. All right, I'll take a dozen, please."

"Excellent choice." Grinning, Jack carefully selected an array of truffles and placed them in an elegant gift box. As he handed it over to the customer, he caught Rosie's eye and winked.

"Thank you, young man," the woman said, paying for her purchase. "These will make her day, I'm sure of it."

"And thank you for choosing the Snowflake Sugar Shop," Jack replied. "I hope your granddaughter has a wonderful birthday."

As the door closed behind the satisfied customer, Rosie raised an eyebrow at Jack. "Well, I must admit, that was pretty impressive."

"Thank you," Jack said. "Never underestimate a Kringle's charm."

The bell above the door chimed as another customer entered. Jack noticed the tension in

Rosie's shoulders as she watched him. His determination to serve customers unnerved her, considering he'd only just arrived, but he was determined to prove his worth.

"Good morning, sir," Jack greeted the newcomer with a bright smile. "What can I get for you today?"

"Uh, I'm not sure," the man hesitated, eyeing the array of sweets on display. "I'm looking for something unique."

"Unique, you say?" Jack mused, rubbing his chin thoughtfully. He glanced over at Rosie, who appeared to be holding her breath, and an idea suddenly came to him. "How about a chocolate brownie pop with one of our famous jelly buttons inside?"

"Sounds interesting," the man said, clearly intrigued. "I'll take six."

"Fantastic. Come back in about fifteen minutes," Jack told him. "These are to be crafted especially for you." He then turned and walked into the workspace. He grabbed the tray of brownies he'd seen cooling on the counter and set to work, ignoring the gaze from Rosie he felt sure would burn a hole right through him. But he refused to let it rattle him. This was his chance to show her he took his job seriously.

He carefully scooped out a portion of brownie, molding it into a perfect sphere before pressing a jelly button inside. Next, he inserted a lollypop stick and dipped it into a bowl of melted chocolate. The deep, rich scent of cocoa filled his nostrils, reminding him of why he had fallen in love with this craft in the first place.

He expertly twirled the brownie pop, ensuring an even coating of chocolate. And while the chocolate would harden on its own, he set them all in the blast chiller for a few minutes.

"Here you are," Jack announced with a flourish, presenting the customer with a box full of six brownie pops. "A Snowflake Sugar Shop exclusive."

The man opened the box and peeked inside. "Wow. They look amazing. Thank you."

"You're welcome." Jack grinned as he watched the customer walk away. "And that's how it's done," he said to Rosie, taking a stage bow.

"I'll agree that how you thought on your feet was pretty clever."

"Thanks," Jack replied. "But you still don't look impressed."

"That'll change if you can whip up another tray of brownies as good as mine. Those were for my book club tonight. We're not a bakery."

"Whoops. Sorry." Jack ran a hand through his hair. Instead of showing what he was capable of, he'd acted impulsively and made things worse. "I didn't realize—"

"I know. But I'll give you a chance to make it up to me. Wow me with some chocolate brownies."

Jack hesitated. Maybe he should cut his losses and be on his way. But if he did, he'd be letting Martin and Sadie down, and despite his lack of interest in joining the Kringle family business, his family was important to him. "No problem," he said. "Get ready to have your tastebuds blown."

At the end of the day, Jack sliced up a tray of brownies, handing Rosie a sample. She took a bite, and he was rewarded with a smile and a begrudging nod of approval.

"If everything you make is as good as these brownies, perhaps this will work out after all."

He grinned and nodded—he was only warming up.

Chapter 4

THE AROMA OF COFFEE filled the air as Rosie took a sip of the latte Jack had given her. She'd forgotten her to-go mug of coffee on the kitchen counter at home that morning, so she welcomed a latte with open arms. Even if it was from Jack.

The jury was still out on Martin's cousin. He'd arrived late, was arrogant, and challenged everything she asked him to do.

So what if he was the handsomest specimen of the male species she'd ever seen? And so what if he had studied in Switzerland, was incredibly talented, fantastic with customers, and looked as if he'd walked a runway in Milan before heading to the store? Working alongside Jack made her feel like a country bumpkin. It didn't help that her mouth went dry, and her brain tied itself in knots every time he gave her a smile.

All she had to do was survive the month. How hard could that be?

Rosie placed her coffee on the counter and picked through a box of heart-shaped decorations. They used these ornaments every year, and she remained convinced that shouldn't change. On the other side of the store was Jack, his attention focused on the laptop as, according to him, the store needed bolder, more modern designs.

He turned the screen toward her. "These glittery pink snowflake decorations will give the shop a unique touch and work cohesively with the silver ones you already have. It will be whimsical and unexpected."

Rosie frowned, her fingers tightening around the vibrant red hearts in her hands. "But it's Valentine's Day we're celebrating, not Christmas. Hearts symbolize love and affection, which is what our customers will expect."

"Except people visit Mistletoe for its Christmas charm all year. And who says snowflakes can't represent love? They're delicate, unique, and beautiful, like love itself."

Good point, Rosie thought as she bit her lip in contemplation. But did they represent warmth and passion as well as belonging? The kind of love that represented a lifetime of stories—the kind she longed for one day? She wasn't entirely convinced snowflakes, even pink ones, represented that. Well, they might to her because of her love of winter, but definitely not to the average person. "I understand your point, but despite the beauty of a snowflake, hearts are more universally recognized as symbols of love.

Our customers will feel more connected to the theme," she insisted.

Jack sighed but said nothing, running a hand through his hair.

What was it about this man that drove her mad? Your crush answered a tiny voice inside her head. What would a worldly chocolatier ever see in a small-town person like you? Rosie shook her head. That was part of it. But she also recognized her reluctance to embrace change and Jack seemed determined to shake things up. "Hearts are a classic symbol of love. They'll draw people in and make them feel the warmth and affection that Valentine's Day is all about."

"Exactly my point," Jack responded, waving a glittery snowflake ornament in the air for emphasis. "Hearts are predictable and overdone. Snowflakes bring a touch of whimsy and uniqueness that our customers will appreciate. I don't understand why you have such unwavering devotion to tradition. Sadie told me you were outgoing and adventurous."

"And Martin told me you'd spent most of your life avoiding commitment. No wonder you don't like what hearts symbolize."

"Ouch," he feigned hurt, placing his hand over his heart. "You get mean when you're wrong."

I'm not mean, Rosie wanted to say. This behavior was so unlike her, but her attraction, combined with the way he brought her frustrations to a boil, resulted in her behaving like a middle-schooler. "I'm not wrong. Our store has always used these hearts. We shouldn't change that because you, an outsider, want something different."

If her earlier comment hadn't hurt him, that one did. They were close enough that she could notice the slightest change in his eyes, indicating that she'd struck a nerve. Oh gosh. Now, she felt even worse.

The sound of the door chime cut through the tension like a heated knife, drawing her attention to the newcomer. Eleanor Frost strode into the shop, her hawk-like eyes immediately noticing the tension between Rosie and Jack.

Her gray hair was pulled back into her signature bun, her lips pressed into a thin line as she took in the scene before her.

"Is everything all right here?" Eleanor asked, raising a judgmental eyebrow at the two of them. The disapproval in her voice hung heavy in the air, causing Rosie to swallow hard, and she noted Jack crossed his arms defensively.

"Everything's fine, Eleanor." Rosie forced a smile onto her face despite the anxiety bubbling up inside her. She knew Eleanor had a knack for gossip, and the last thing she wanted was for their disagreement to become the talk of the town.

"Good," Eleanor said curtly, her gaze lingering on Rosie for a moment longer before she turned her attention to Jack. "And who might you be?"

"This is Martin's cousin, Jack. He's a chocolatier," Rosie answered. "And he's here to help me while Sadie is on her honeymoon."

"Nice to meet you," Jack chimed in, his voice soft and pleasant, but Rosie detected insincerity underneath it. "Please let me know if you require any assistance."

Eleanor gave him a quick nod and then browsed the store. Rosie stood still, not knowing what to do. She couldn't start hanging decorations lest she and Jack start arguing again. Rosie bit her lip, acutely aware of Eleanor's gaze as if it followed her every move. She felt like a mouse under surveillance by a bird of prey. One wrong move and, whoosh, she'd be gone.

Knowing she was overreacting didn't help. Eleanor was an annoying gossip, and until today, Rosie had found the woman's penchant for pessimism sad but occasionally amusing. Why was the woman getting to her? Maybe her blood sugar was too low. Or maybe, just maybe, her fears were correct, and she wasn't cut out to run the store.

The door jingled again, and Caleb Winters walked in. Never had Rosie been so glad to see her friend. He stepped into the store with a grin, but she noticed it falter slightly, and Rosie assumed he had picked up on the tension. He raised his eyebrows, and she slightly nodded in Eleanor's direction.

"Ah," he said, winking at her. "Well, good morning everyone." His cheerful voice boomed across the store. "And you must be Jack." Caleb walked over to where Jack was standing. "I'm Caleb. I own the general store across the square. Nice to meet you."

"Likewise," said Jack and extended his hand for a shake.

"And what do we have here?" Eleanor interrupted, tapping on a display case. She pointed to a chocolate heart covered in a red and pink marbleized mirror glaze. "They're new, aren't they? What makes you think people will buy these over the classics?"

"Jack made them," Rosie said, trying to keep her tone light and friendly. "He trained in Switzerland, so you know they'll be good."

"Switzerland, hmm?" Eleanor mused, raising a thinly plucked eyebrow. "Well, I suppose we'll have to see if his fancy training is worth anything, won't we?"

Jack stiffened, and Rosie quickly placed a hand on his arm. "Now, wait a second, Eleanor," she said. Rosie refused to let anyone make unfounded criticisms about her store or her employees--especially one as talented as Jack. "How dare you come into my shop and criticize our products without having tasted a single one? I'll have you know Jack is an extraordinary chocolatier, and the town of Mistletoe is lucky to have him for the next month. If you're not going to buy anything, I suggest you be on your way."

Rosie's heart pounded in her chest, and blood rushed past her ears. Never in her life had she spoken to a customer in such a manner.

Eleanor pursed her lips, clearly not pleased with Rosie's attitude, but she had no counter-argument. "Very well," she said stiffly. "But I'll be keeping a close eye on things as always." And with that, she turned on her heel and left the shop, leaving Rosie, Jack, and Caleb to breathe a collective sigh of relief.

"Who was that ray of sunshine?" Jack asked.

"That was Eleanor Frost," Caleb said. "Town gossip."

"Frost, huh? Interesting," Jack said. "She's certainly cold."

Caleb shrugged. "We're all pretty good at ignoring her snide comments. That's why I'm so surprised to see her get to you like that, Rosie."

"Me too. I used to tell Sadie to ignore her. Now I'm the one getting upset. Sadie was right. She looks at you as if expecting you to fail. It's unnerving."

"And untrue," Caleb said. "Especially for the Snowflake Sugar Shop. You guys are doing so well, particularly your online business."

Rosie smiled at her friend. "I know, but I'm feeling the pressure with Sadie out of town."

"Don't listen to that old woman," Jack said. "Your candy is delicious. And even if people are uncertain about my skills, they know you'd never sell anything below your high standards."

"You think so?" The compliment surprised Rosie, and a flush of heat filled her cheeks.

"He's right," Caleb agreed, offering her a reassuring smile, his brown eyes warm and kind. "So the reason I came by is to tell you the red lights you ordered will arrive in the next day or two."

"Perfect, thanks. We were just discussing the decorations," Rosie said, turning to Jack. "With that much red, perhaps we can use the silver and pink snowflakes. The red will reflect off them, sending color throughout the store. What do you think, Caleb?"

"I think it's my cue to leave," he replied, turning toward the door. "I'm sure anything you do will look great, Rosie. It always does." And with that, he walked out, the shop falling silent.

"Look," Jack said, moving closer to Rosie. "I can be stubborn. I'm sorry. This is your store, not mine."

"Thank you," Rosie said. "And I can be stuck in my ways. Let's wait for the lights to arrive because I'll admit, I like the idea of snowflakes reflecting the red lights, kind of like disco balls, and snowflake is part of our name, so it all goes together."

"But so do the hearts. What if we strung them among the snowflakes—wait! I've got it. What if we hang the snowflakes in the shape of a heart?"

"That's a great idea."

"So we've come to a compromise?"

"I believe we have." Rosie smiled. They were both talented confectioners. If they could work together, Rosie had no doubt they would develop some unique candy creations. All she had to do was forget about her crush because a guy like Jack would never be interested in a woman like her—but friendship? She could do that. She had to do that. Otherwise, they were in for a long, long month.

Chapter 5

"ALRIGHT, LET'S SEE... HEART-SHAPED lollipops, check," Rosie murmured, crossing items off her inventory list with a flourish. Her fingers brushed against a stack of decorative ribbons, reminding her of the garnishing needed for the gift boxes, and she scribbled a note on her list.

"Good day to you, Rosie," a customer called out, entering the shop. "I need two dozen of those love potion jelly candies for my wife's bridge night. Can you have them ready by to-morrow?"

"Of course, Mr. Williams. I'll get right on it." Rosie scribbled down the order in her note-book. She flashed him a cheerful smile as he left, and she hurried to the kitchen, already calcu-lating how much sugar and gelatin she would need.

As she carefully measured the ingredients, Rosie couldn't help but feel the responsibility weighing on her shoulders. A sudden pang of longing for her parents' guidance washed over her, but she quickly brushed it aside. Now was not the time for nostalgia; there were orders to fill and inventory to manage and—the door chimed cheerfully, announcing the arrival of a new customer. Luckily, she was at a point where she could leave the sugar simmering for a few minutes. It was silly to have made this while alone in the shop. Another reason to question her management abilities.

Rosie walked out from the back to find Mayor Gregory Evergreen wearing one of his trademark Christmas suits. The mayor's enthusiasm over Mistletoe's Christmas village theme was unparalleled.

"Good afternoon, Mayor Evergreen. What can I help you with today?"

Mayor Evergreen strode toward the counter, his eyes scanning the shop as he took in the organized chaos that surrounded Rosie. "Well, my dear Miss Plum, I'm just checking in, and I must say, it does look like you're handling quite the workload. Are you sure you can manage all this on your own?"

Though she tried to maintain her cheerful demeanor, she felt both a twinge of insecurity and a twinge of anger at the mayor's pointed question. She plastered on a confident smile. "Of course."

"I hope so. Sadie is a seasoned business-woman," Mayor Evergreen countered, his skepticism evident in his furrowed brow. "The Valentine season must be the busiest time of year for the shop, and I'm not sure it's wise for you to be tackling everything alone."

Rosie's cheeks flushed with indignation. When Sadie arrived in Mistletoe, she was hardly a seasoned businesswoman. Rosie had far more experience at running the shop than Sadie did. And before Rosie had been made a partner in the business, no one doubted her abilities, as she'd worked tirelessly to ensure the shop's success. But this wasn't about her abilities; this was about her past—her family's past.

"Mayor Evergreen, I appreciate your concern, but I assure you, I am more than capable of managing the shop. I worked side by side with Mable for years before Sadie arrived, learning the ins and outs of this business," she replied, her voice firm yet respectful, or so she hoped. Her own self-doubt was one thing. Outwardly, no reason existed to warrant concern.

Mayor Evergreen studied her for a moment, his expression unreadable. Finally, he nodded slowly as if conceding to her determination. "Very well, Rosie," he said, smiling thinly. "I trust you'll give it your all. And remember, the success of this shop affects our entire community."

"I'm well aware, Mayor Evergreen." Taking a calming breath, Rosie wondered why there weren't more pressing town matters to be concerned with. "Now, if you'll excuse me, I have some sugar on the stove."

She made it to the back as the door jingled, announcing the mayor's departure, leaving Rosie alone. She glanced at the candy thermometer. It wasn't quite at the right temperature yet. Suddenly, her eyes blurred as a mixture of frustration and sadness welled up inside her. She clenched her fists as she blinked back tears, releasing a shaky breath.

"Mom, Dad, I could really use your strength right now," she whispered, her voice cracking.

A warm memory washed over her like a comforting blanket—her parents' laughter filling their kitchen, the smell of freshly baked cookies wafting through the air. Rosie had always been happiest when they were all together at the bakery, creating sweet treats that brought smiles to people's faces. It had been more than a business to her parents; it was their family legacy, their love woven into every delicious bite.

"Rosie, my dear," her mother's gentle voice echoed in her mind, "remember that you are never alone. We're always with you."

Tears welled up in Rosie's eyes as the memory faded, replaced by the smell of burning sugar. "Oh no," Rosie cried, removing the pot from the element. "I'm going to have to start over." That wasn't her only problem. The store smelled like smoke—hardly an inviting aroma to customers—so she opened the back door and waved a tea towel to ventilate it.

She was shutting the door when her cell phone rang. It was Sadie. What timing. "Why hello, Sadie."

"Hi, Rosie," Sadie's voice sounded far away.

"Is everything okay?" Rosie asked.

"Absolutely perfect." Sadie's love for Martin came through loud and clear. "But enough about me. How are you holding up with the shop?"

"Good. Everything is good," Rosie said. Aside from the burned sugar and her own insecurities, everything was going well.

"And how is it working with Jack? He's kind of cute, isn't he?"

Wait. What? "Working with Jack is fine, and I've been too busy to notice things like that," Rosie lied. Of course, she'd noticed. In fact, she was pretty sure every woman in town had noticed. Two women entered the store that morning, and when they discovered Jack wasn't there, they left without buying anything.

"Is he there? Martin wants a word."

"No. He stepped out for a moment." Ellie had called with an issue at Martin's toy store requiring Jack's help, but Rosie didn't want them to worry. "I'll pass on the message. Enjoy your honeymoon."

"You're amazing, Rosie. Thank you for taking such good care of our little store."

"Anytime," Rosie assured her. "Now go have fun, and don't worry about a thing."

"You too, my friend, and take your own advice."

With that, the line went dead, leaving Rosie alone once more with her thoughts, her doubts, and an ever-growing pile of work. But Sadie's comments had given her pause. Sadie and Martin wouldn't have had Jack come to work there as a set-up, would they? No. That wasn't their style, but people in love tended to want everyone to be in love. And other than the art of confection, what did she and Jack have in common? Nothing, as far as she knew.

And he wasn't merely cute. The man was gorgeous. So much so that he was way out of Rosie's league. He was stunning no matter what he did, washing dishes, melting chocolate, and oh, when he had an apron over his black sweater and blue jeans, with cocoa powder smeared on his cheek...She shook her head, clearing the image from her mind. They were colleagues. Maybe even friends. Still, there was no harm in—

"Haydee ho," Nora Kringle called out as she entered the store, startling Rosie. "I'm here like I promised. What happened with Uncle Jack today? How come he had to leave?" she asked as she removed her coat. "And what's that smell?"

Rosie chuckled at the stream of questions. "As far as Jack is concerned, Ellie called moments after he arrived, needing him at the toy store. He didn't say why. And I'm sorry to text you while you were at school to ask if you could work, but I'm grateful for your help. Especially since I now need to make some candy for Mrs. William's bridge night. I've already burned one batch, hence the smell. If you could serve any customers that come in, I should be able to work undistracted."

"No problem," Nora said and selected an apron.

The afternoon wore on. Rosie had finished making the candy and was chatting to Nora as they packaged an online order when a customer entered. The store closed in ten minutes, and after an exhausting day, Rosie hoped she wouldn't take too long to decide.

"Good afternoon," Rosie said cheerfully. "Welcome to the Snowflake Sugar Shop. How can we help you?"

The woman turned to Rosie. She had jet black hair cut into a short bob, dramatic eyeliner, and bright red lips, smiling awkwardly. "I would like to speak to Sadie Kringle."

"Sorry. She's not here, and she won't be back for a few weeks. Is there anything I can help you with?"

"I'm in town to work on a story," the woman said while studying a candy display. "I heard Mistletoe underwent a huge transformation last year."

"Yes, that's right," Rosie said, wiping her hands.

"And Sadie was a big part of that, correct?"

"Yes," Rosie said, uncomfortable where the conversation was going. "Why do you want to know?"

"It's quite an unusual change, don't you think? Proposing that a town way up here become a tourist destination. One based on Christmas, no less."

"Not really. We were already known for our light festival. And, of course, Santa lives up north, so it all makes sense, even though we're hardly the North Pole." Rosie glanced at Nora, who made an odd sound.

"Santa. Exactly," the woman said, surprising Rosie with a smug smile. "So tell me, do you know if Sadie knew the Kringles prior to moving here?"

"Sorry, but I don't disclose personal information to strangers. Now, we're closing up, so if you're not here to buy candy, I would like it if you let us get to our duties."

"Of course," the woman said, then reached into her purse. "But here is my card. If you think of anything you'd like to tell me about the town's recent changes, please call."

Rosie took the card. "Have a good night."

The woman spun on what Rosie deemed very inappropriate winter footwear for Alaska and exited the store.

"Is it just me, or was that an odd conversation?" She turned to Nora. The typically sassy teen had remained unusually quiet.

"It was definitely odd," Nora eventually agreed. "And to be honest with you, I have a bad feeling about it."

Rosie nodded, worried about Sadie. Her friend had an unpleasant experience on a reality show a couple of years back, but Rosie didn't think that was why the woman was there. With a shrug, Rosie dropped the woman's business card into the junk drawer underneath the cash register.

They quickly cleaned up and closed the store. Nora took off for home like a bullet instead of hanging around to chat as usual. Was the girl concerned about why Jack was called into her father's toy store? Perhaps, but she'd seemed okay until the reporter had shown up. Whatever it was, it filled Rosie with unease, and she couldn't help but agree with Nora—she had a bad feeling, too.

Chapter 6

TWINKLING FAIRY LIGHTS DRAPED along the wooden beams of Martin and Sadie's kitchen cast a gentle sparkle onto the rustic furnishings below, and Jack chuckled inwardly at Martin for keeping up a few nods to Christmas in late January. That man was a Kringle through and through.

"Pass the potatoes, please?" Nora asked.

"Of course, Nora." Jack playfully slid the bowl across the table toward her. As he did so, he caught a glimpse of the family photos that adorned the mantelpiece, reminding him of his legendary roots and the importance of the bonds the Kringle family shared—bonds that didn't include him.

"You know," Ellie began, taking the bowl from Nora and serving herself some potatoes, "it's really nice to see you settling in here, Jack. Even if it's only for a little while."

Jack smiled at Ellie. Ever the observant one, she must have noticed the moment of reflection that flickered across Jack's face. Having spent considerable time together in their youth, Ellie knew how Jack's differences made him feel like an outsider in his family. "Yeah," he said, meeting her gaze. "But pretty soon your boys are going to wonder why you're always eating dinner with us."

"Oh heck, don't worry about them. My husband is picking up pizza after their hockey practice, and the less time I spend around stinky hockey bags, the better."

"Well, it's nice to know I rate above sweaty hockey equipment," Jack teased, and they all laughed.

As the conversation flowed effortlessly between them, the coziness of the cabin wrapped itself around Jack's shoulders like a warm blanket, offering him solace and an unfamiliar sense of belonging amidst the uncertainty that lay ahead. Uncertainty caused by his trip to the toy workshop that afternoon.

"So why did you need Uncle Jack at the toy store today?" Nora asked Ellie as if she could read his mind.

Ellie glanced at Jack, her brow furrowing in concern.

"What?" Nora asked. "Now you have me worried."

"Nothing's wrong with the store or workshop or anyone who works for us. But we received this mysterious letter. And it was somewhat unsettling," Ellie told her.

Nora placed her fork and knife on the table. "What did it say?"

"It was only two words, all in caps. 'I KNOW.' Just the way it was written was ominous," Jack said.

"What does that mean?" Nora asked. "Do they know about us?"

"Don't panic," Ellie said. "This kind of thing has happened before. It usually blows over."

"Usually?" Nora's panic was obvious in the pitch of her voice.

"It could be anything," Jack added, hoping to ease her fears. "Nothing at all to do with our family magic."

"You're not making me feel better. Did you tell Dad?"

"Martin doesn't need to know yet. Let him enjoy his honeymoon in peace," Jack said.

"We've emailed your great-grandfather, your grandfather, and all the other workshops as a heads-up. But we're not that worried," added Ellie.

"Worried enough that Jack was called away from Snowflake Sugar," Nora continued.

"Well, we do have to be careful," Jack said. "But that doesn't mean we have to panic." He reached across the table and squeezed Nora's arm. She was as white as a ghost. "Are you okay?"

"I don't know." Nora stared at her dinner plate. "Something weird happened today at the store."

"Weird?" Jack asked. "Don't tell me Rosie was in a good mood."

"That's not funny," Nora said, and Jack noticed her eyes growing moist. "This woman came in. She said she's a reporter, and then she began asking strange questions about Sadie and Mistletoe."

Jack stiffened in his chair, and he glanced at Ellie. "What kind of questions?"

Nora shrugged. "About Sadie being part of the town's big change and if she knew our family before moving here and isn't it weird to live in a Christmas village all year and stuff."

"What did you tell her?"

"Nothing. But then Rosie made a joke about Santa, and I could tell that got her attention.

Finally, Rosie asked her to leave if she wasn't going to buy anything."

Jack's stomach dropped. This was too much of a coincidence, but he didn't want to alarm Nora. "I'm sure it's not related at all. But thanks for telling us."

"Absolutely," said Ellie. "I'll tell the team leaders about a nosy reporter in town, so they are on high alert."

"Good idea. And I'll try to find out what else this reporter wants and who she's talking to," Jack added.

"We have her card," Nora said. "Rosie stuck it in the drawer under the cash register."

Jack nodded. Good. He would begin re-searching the researcher. In the meantime, he wanted to ease some of Nora's worries, especially since her father was out of town.

"Remember a few years ago, before I left to study, I wanted to amaze you all with my candy-making skills."

"I remember," said Ellie. "Don't you Nora?"

"If you mean those sugar-coated monstrosities, yes I do," Nora laughed, and it filled Jack with relief to see the girl's tension ease.

"Hey now," Jack protested playfully, tossing a napkin at Nora. "I may not have succeeded in making traditional candy canes, but those sugar-coated monstrosities still tasted pretty good."

"Once you dipped them in chocolate," Nora said.

"See. That shows you I made the right career choice," Jack said.

"True," agreed Ellie, raising her glass in mock tribute. "To unconventional confectioners and the people who love them."

"Cheers," Nora and Jack chimed in, clinking their glasses together and sharing a moment of laughter. But even amidst the lighthearted banter, a subtle undercurrent of tension remained. Jack could feel it, and he suspected the others could, too. But for now, all they could do was wait.

·♥·♥·♥·♥·♥·

Jack was finishing up the dinner dishes when Nora entered the kitchen. She poured a glass of water and then sat at the kitchen island.

"Finished your homework?" Jack asked.

"Yeah." Nora wiped at the condensation on the glass.

"Something on your mind, kiddo? I mean, besides the letter?"

"I guess. It's Rosie."

"What about her?"

"I think she had been crying today—not in front of me, but her eyes were red when I arrived at work."

"What? Are you sure? Because I wasn't there?"

"No. Of course not. Wow. You have quite the ego. But seriously, we were fine. She was actually more like her old self when we were busy. She talked about her parents a few times. I don't know. Maybe she misses them."

"They're not local?"

"They used to live closer to Anchorage, but her parents are deceased."

"Both of them?"

"That's what Sadie told me," Nora shrugged. "I don't know. Maybe it has nothing to do with it. Maybe I caught her having a bad moment because she burned some sugar—which also isn't like her. But she hasn't been herself for a while."

"Running a business is hard."

"I guess," Nora sighed. "But I miss her unwavering optimism and how much fun we had. I don't think she's gone skating yet this year. Last year we went tons of times after work."

"Rosie enjoys skating?"

"Are you kidding me? She likes everything to do with winter. In fact, I've never met anyone who loves winter more. Except maybe you. Hey, can you do something to cheer her up? Something fun? Maybe even something magical?"

"Now is not a smart time to use magic."

"I know, but I bet that reporter is looking for Santa magic. Dude, you're Jack Frost. It's already winter. No one would notice."

"Okay, first of all, don't call me Jack Frost. Especially after having met that cranky busybody in town. Second, if no one would notice, why bother?"

"Okay, okay, even if you don't use your magic, take her to do something fun."

"I don't think she likes me."

"That's ridiculous. You both have so much in common."

"Not really."

"Oh yeah? How about your devotion to confection? Your love of snow? And you're both stubborn perfectionists."

Jack thought about Rosie's bright green eyes and her determination. Things would be so much better if they had common ground and got along. "I'll think about it."

"Yay. Thanks, Uncle Jack," Nora said, jumping off the stool and wrapping him in a hug. "Now, how about a mug of your famous hot chocolate?"

"Right before bed? How can you tolerate all that sugar?"

"I'm not an old man like you."

"Hey watch it, kiddo."

"Joking. You know that."

Jack made her the drink and Nora left to play video games online with her friends, leaving him alone, for which he was grateful. He needed time to think. If the letter was indeed about Santa's workshop, they might be in more trouble than he wanted to admit. Yet despite his efforts to think of a plan, his mind kept returning to a certain candy maker who apparently loved winter as much as he did.

Chapter 7

Rosie paced back and forth behind the counter of the Snowflake Sugar Shop. The scent of sugar and cream filled the air, but it did nothing to soothe her frayed nerves. She glanced at the ruined batch of candy on the counter, her bright green eyes filling with dismay. No matter how hard she tried, the caramel refused to set correctly, turning into an unmanageable sticky mess.

"Alright, Rosie," she muttered under her breath. "You can do this. You've fixed worse before." Her hands trembled slightly as she picked up the caramel-covered wooden spoon, willing herself to remain optimistic despite the gnawing feeling of stress.

"Who am I kidding? This is a disaster." She put her head down and cried. Right then, Jack strode into the shop.

She lifted her head, only to find that she had caramel in her hair. Could the day get any worse?

"Hey, Rosie," Jack greeted her warmly. "I'd ask how it's going, but I'm going to hazard a guess that you've had better mornings."

"Wow. You should be a detective," Rosie said, struggling to keep her voice steady. "It's...well, I'm having a bit of trouble with this caramel." She made her way to the sink, desperate to get the caramel out of her hair.

Jack approached the counter, his brows knitting together in concern as he studied the situation. No doubt he could see the stress etched in the lines around her eyes, the tension likely radiating off her like a heatwave. It was as if the self-inflicted anxiety she'd been shouldering since Sadie left for her honeymoon could no longer be contained.

"Here. Let me help," he said gently, placing a reassuring hand on her arm. "We all have off days."

Rosie hesitated momentarily, her pride warring with the exhaustion that threatened to overtake her. But as she met Jack's steady gaze, something in his eyes made her feel safe and protected. She nodded gratefully, releasing a breath she hadn't realized she'd been holding.

"Thank you, Jack," she said. "I really appreciate it."

He flashed her a sincere smile, then proceeded to find a clean cloth and soap it up. "Sit."

Rosie sat on a stool, amazed by Jack's tender touch as he carefully extracted the sticky sweetness from her hair, his fingers skillfully navigating through her mass of spirals. Each gentle tug brought their faces closer, and Rosie noticed the finer details of his face—the crinkles around his eyes that told stories of laughter, the way his hair fell slightly over his brow, and the sincere concern in his gaze as if performing the most delicate of surgeries.

Their breaths mingled, causing her heart to race. The air was thick with the aroma of caramel, yet she could make out the scent of Jack's aftershave, a subtle indicator of the cozy world they momentarily created. And in the quiet intimacy of the candy store, Jack was no longer the arrogant chocolatier she happened to have a crush on but a man whose careful touches and soft glances spoke of a deeper connection.

"There, all done," Jack said, shattering their cozy bubble, and Rosie's dream-like thoughts crashed to the ground in pieces like a dropped sugar ornament.

"I don't know what's wrong with me," she said softly.

"Everyone makes mistakes," Jack replied.

"Not me. Not with candy, anyway. I've wasted more supplies with careless errors this week than in the past year."

"Maybe you need a break."

"Yeah. I guess, but I can't go on vacation until Sadie returns."

"That's not exactly what I meant, although you should do that all the same. What I meant was…Nora told me you enjoy skating."

"I love skating," Rosie said. How she missed the freedom of gliding across the ice.

"So then, what are we waiting for? You've been working nonstop since Sadie left. You deserve a break, and I know a perfect spot nearby."

Rosie bit her lip, torn between the tempting offer and her sense of duty toward the shop. She'd always found comfort in being surrounded by the sugary scents and cheerful glow of the Snowflake Sugar Shop, but lately, it felt like the weight of the world was pressing down on her shoulders.

"Jack, that sounds amazing, but I can't leave. There's too much to do, plus the mess with the caramel."

"Rosie, listen to me." Jack's voice softened as he looked into her eyes. "You're not doing yourself any favors by running yourself ragged. You need to take care of yourself, too. Trust me, everything will be just fine here for a little while. It's Wednesday. The shop doesn't open until noon. We have two hours until then."

Her fingers traced the edge of the sticky caramel disaster before her as she mulled over his words. The inviting image of gliding on ice flickered in her mind, tugging at her heart. It had been ages since she'd done something for herself, and the thought of spending some time outside the shop was both thrilling and terrifying.

"Are you sure?" she finally asked, her voice wavering with uncertainty.

"Absolutely," Jack reassured her, giving her arm a gentle squeeze. "And when we return, we'll tackle this caramel situation together."

Rosie hesitated for another moment, then slowly nodded. She knew deep down that Jack was right. She needed to take a step back, even if only for a short while, and allow herself the chance to recharge. "Okay," she agreed. "Let's go ice skating."

"Great." Jack's face lit up with excitement, his eyes twinkling like the first snowflakes of winter. "Now, let's go get your skates."

"No need. I have two pairs. One I keep here and one I keep at home."

"Wow. Nora was right. You really do like skating."

"I do. What about your skates?"

"Mine are in the sleigh."

"You brought the Kringle sleigh? And you have your skates?"

Jack grinned. "First of all, since I'm staying at Martin's, I get to use all his toys, including the sleigh, and second, I enjoy skating, too. If there's a patch of ice, I'll skate on it."

This made Rosie laugh. And as she bundled up for their morning skate, she felt a spark of excitement igniting within her. Perhaps this was exactly what she needed.

With that one laugh, Rosie underwent a transformation as breathtaking as it was instantaneous. It was as if her laughter had the power to banish every shadow that dared to linger on her features. Her face now shone with a radiance that could rival the brilliance of sunlight reflecting off a pristine snowscape. The lines of stress that had previously marred her expression melted away, leaving a visage of pure joy and unbridled playfulness in their place. In that unguarded moment of laughter, Rosie embodied the essence of light-heartedness and whimsy, a stark contrast to the more subdued persona she usually presented to Jack.

This was the Rosie that Nora and Martin had told him about.

Impulsively, Jack took her hand and led her behind the store where the sleigh and elk awaited. Jack released her hand, climbed into the sleigh, and offered his hand again.

"Aren't you just getting your skates?" Rosie asked.

"Nope. I thought we'd take the sleigh."

"But we can walk to the skating rink."

"I know of a spot better than that."

"You do? How?"

"Just because I don't live here doesn't mean I don't go exploring. Besides, winter is my favorite time to explore."

"Mine too," Rosie agreed, then accepted Jack's hand and climbed aboard.

They made their way out of town, soon approaching a nearby lake.

"Here we are," Jack announced, a mischievous smile playing on his lips as he surveyed the scene before them. "It's perfect."

Surrounded by tall pines heavy with soft snow, they could just make out the frozen lake.

"Wait here. I'm going to make sure the ice is safe."

"I'm sure it's fine, but it might be a bit bumpy."

"Let me check. It will make me feel better."

"Sure, suit yourself. I'm quite comfortable in the sleigh. No wonder Sadie loves riding in it," Rosie said and pulled a blanket across her lap.

Jack made his way down to the lake. It was small, more of a pond, nestled amidst the rugged Alaskan wilderness. And Rosie had been correct. The surface was indeed bumpy, with some spots laden with snow too deep to skate in.

Jack glanced up toward the sleigh, ensuring Rosie remained there. Then he laid his hand on the ice, closed his eyes, and opened his mind. The snow blew off the surface, fringing the pond, while the ice surface smoothed out and became so clear you could see the rocks and branches trapped below the surface.

When the scene was as he wanted, he returned to the sleigh. "All good. Let's go."

They grabbed their skates and headed down to the pond. Rosie gasped, and Jack smiled as her mouth fell open into the cutest 'O.'

"I've never seen...how did you find such a place? I mean, look at the ice, it's so smooth, and I can see into the water. Are you sure it's safe?"

"Absolutely. I'm glad you like it."

"Like it? I love it. It's absolutely majestic. You know, I've never understood how people grumble and complain about winter. I mean, sure, storms cause problems, but you can say the same about a summer rainstorm."

Heat flooded Jack's chest. Finally, he'd met someone who appreciated winter's beauty as much as he did. "Winter is often perceived as the harshest of seasons, but I find it holds within it an unmatched beauty. And not merely in its visual splendor but in the experiences it offers. It's in the crisp air that rejuvenates the spirit, the joy of seeing one's breath materialize in little puffs of vapor, and the cozy warmth of retreating into a snug space after being out in the cold. Winter's beauty is in the stark contrasts—the bright whiteness of snow against the deep greens of evergreens, the silent, frozen lakes and rivers, and the stark, bare branches of deciduous trees creating intricate silhouettes against the winter sky."

"Wow," Rosie whispered. "That was surprisingly eloquent and so, so true. You seem to have expressed exactly how I see it, too. Growing up in Alaska, winter is accepted as a way of life, but I don't know how many people truly love and appreciate it."

Jack grinned. "I guess we have two things in common now: confection and winter."

"I guess we do." Rosie laughed, sending a fiery bolt straight into Jack's heart.

"Well, let's get going then. We don't have much time," said Jack, secretly wishing they could spend hours there together.

They made their way to the ice and sat on a log that Jack cleared of snow, lacing up their skates.

"Ready?" Jack asked, offering his hand to Rosie.

"Ready as I'll ever be." Rosie took his hand with a grin.

They stepped onto the ice and began gliding gracefully. Jack watched as Rosie skated across the pond, each stride with the beauty of a ballerina and a smile as bright as the sun. Beyond the pond, the evergreen trees stood covered in snow, and the ground, untouched and pristine save for a few animal tracks, sparkled under the clear blue sky. In the background stood the rugged Alaskan mountains, and the silence of the wilderness was only broken by the sound of their blades. Even his magic couldn't compete with the majesty of an Alaskan winter. But most of all, nothing could compare to the awe-inspiring beauty of his auburn-haired companion as she glided around in the perfect blend of peace and exhilaration as if she were the embodiment of the perfect winter day.

Rosie glided over the frozen lake, her skates carving elegant arcs on the glassy surface. The crisp air nipped at her cheeks, but inside, she felt a warmth. Each stroke of her blades was a stroke of freedom, a release from the confines of daily life.

With each turn and spin, Rosie felt a rush of exhilaration. She felt alive, her spirit soaring as high as the birds that watched from their perches in the trees. In these moments, nothing else mattered but the sheer joy of movement, the thrill of speed, and the boundless freedom that came with being one with the ice. It was as if she was the only person in the world, alone with the elements, communing with the icy wind, the clear blue sky, the frozen pond, and the solid earth beneath layers of snow.

But she wasn't alone. She was with Jack, and they were skating together. All thanks to him. This had been exactly what she needed. Why hadn't she seen that? She'd been so focused on the store that she'd done more harm than good. She now felt refreshed and recharged.

She'd find the strength to forget about her crush—something this afternoon would make more challenging but necessary. If they worked together, they could make this Valentine's season an outstanding success.

Rosie skated up to Jack. "Tell you what, we have to get back soon, but how about once around the pond? Loser buys lattes."

"Deal," he said, then extended his hand. She took it, but instead of the expected handshake, he skated ahead and then launched her in front. "Go," he yelled.

Rosie laughed so hard that she could hardly skate, but she didn't care who won. Jack had already given her a precious gift.

Chapter 8

ROSIE LEFT CALEB'S STORE, a role of sturdy, translucent fishing line in her hand. This was perfect for hanging the decorations in the candy store's front window, and she could already visualize the delicate shimmering snowflakes suspended like magical ornaments. The sun bathed the morning with a radiant glow, its beams caressing her face as she turned upwards, her lips curving into a contented smile, enjoying the perfection of the winter day.

As she made her way across the town square, Rosie's steps were light, as if dancing to an inaudible melody. She approached the majestic Christmas tree, standing tall all year long, proudly serving as the centerpiece of Mistletoe. At least the decorations were seasonal. The green and red balls and candy canes that adorned it at Christmas were now replaced by red heart ornaments. March would be shamrocks, and April would be pastel egg ornaments. She chuckled. There was no end to how one could decorate a Christmas tree.

It was then that Rosie heard the unmistakable timbre of Eleanor Frost's voice, a sound that made her pause mid-step. Her mind raced. Should she retreat and take another path or summon the courage to face the woman?

Before she came to a decision, she heard the deep, authoritative voice of Mayor Evergreen. His words floated through the air, speaking fondly of Sadie and Martin. "Ay, yes, the

Kringles," he mused, his voice full of respect. "They've truly become pillars of our community. Without their vision and spirit, I doubt we'd see the prosperity we enjoy today. It was Sadie's brilliant idea, after all, that sparked the transformation of Mistletoe from an economically challenged town to the tourist destination you witness today."

"Hmm," came a third, distinctively sharp voice, cutting through the air like a well-aimed arrow. Rosie's hand flew to her mouth in a reflex of surprise and recognition. That unmistakable tone belonged to the keen-eyed reporter who had visited the candy store a few days prior. What was this reporter piecing together?

"And you're certain Sadie never knew Martin Kringle before her arrival here?" the reporter probed, her voice laced with skepticism and intrigue.

Mayor Evergreen, with a tone of patient explanation, said, "Yes, absolutely certain. But I fail to see how this ties into your piece about Mistletoe. What's the relevance?"

The reporter's voice softened yet remained firm. "Well, I'm attempting to weave together the threads of the town's evolution. Understanding the key players and their backstory adds depth to the narrative of change, don't you think?"

When her question was met with silence, she continued. "Regarding the Kringles, would you say there's anything...out of the ordinary about their family?"

It pleased Rosie that the mayor's immediate response was tinged with a protective edge. "Unusual? Now, Ms. Mitchell, this line of questioning is veering dangerously close to tabloid territory, far from the respectful article on our town's transformation I was expecting."

Eleanor, of course, couldn't resist chiming in. "Come now, Gregory. Let's not be too hasty. There's no harm in indulging a little of our local lore for an interested journalist. After all, it's no secret that Martin Kringle has been at the center of quite a few whispers and rumors since his arrival."

Rosie had heard enough. The thought of Eleanor Frost gossiping about her friends was intolerable. With a surge of protective resolve, she emerged from behind the Christmas tree with determination.

"Mayor Evergreen, Eleanor, how nice to see you both on this beautiful day," she greeted, hoping her voice carried a melody of courtesy.

"Indeed," responded Mayor Evergreen, his demeanor embodying his typical warmth and geniality. "And how are things at the Snowflake Sugar Shop?"

"Splendid, thank you," Rosie said.

"Let me introduce you to Ava Mitchell." The mayor motioned toward the reporter. "She's writing an article on the transformation of Mistletoe."

Eleanor, never one to miss a beat, added, "Rosie works closely with Sadie."

"Yes, we've met before," said Rosie. "She came into the shop the other day, asking all sorts of questions about Sadie and Martin. Remind me, what publication are you with again?"

Ava Mitchell's composure momentarily faltered, her face tightening. "I work freelance," she finally said. "I intend to present the piece to various outlets."

The mayor's expression subtly shifted, a flicker of realization crossing his features. Apparently, he had never inquired about her affiliation, and with no apparent immediate benefits to the town, his patience waned.

"It sounds like there is something specific you wanted to know about the Kringle family," Mayor Evergreen said, his usually warm voice adopting a more formal, guarded tone. "The Kringle family is an important part of this community, and I'd hate to see their reputation tarnished by unfounded rumors. If you wish to discuss the town further, I suggest making an appointment. Otherwise, I'd prefer not to be approached informally in public. Good day, ladies."

Mayor Evergreen gave the three women a curt nod and then proceeded toward city hall.

"We should probably get going too, shouldn't we, Eleanor?" Rosie gave the woman a tight-lipped smile.

"Oh, yes, very well," Eleanor replied, feigning disinterest. "I have far more important things to do with my time than stand around and gossip."

Rosie stifled a laugh as Eleanor turned on her heel and marched off.

"Well then, Ms. Plum," the reporter said, and Rosie picked up an edge of challenge in her tone. "It appears you've scared off my interview subjects. What are you afraid of?"

"Spiders mostly. Oh, and snakes. Something about the way they wiggle unnerves me," she quipped. Her smile then faded into seriousness. "But as far as your questions go, fear isn't the issue. I do, however, take offense at your apparent intention of digging up dirt on my friends. I simply won't stand for that."

"You think you know them so well? Wait and see Ms. Plum. Wait and see."

Rosie gave the woman a nonchalant shrug and then continued to the candy store. Her feet had succumbed to the cold despite her large boots, and her previous enthusiasm for creating the Valentine's Day display had diminished. But what weighed most heavily on Rosie's heart was an inexplicable feeling of unease. It was as if a shadow had crept over her morning. A sense of disquiet gnawed at her, a subtle but persistent thought that not everything was as it seemed. With each step toward the candy store, Rosie couldn't shake off the feeling, and it settled uncomfortably in the pit of her stomach.

Chapter 9

J ACK NEVER HAD TROUBLE sleeping, but last night had proven to be an exception. The reporter that had been snooping around Mistletoe consumed his mind. Not to mention the ominous letter. Having devoted the majority of his adult life to traveling rather than participating in the family business, he usually steered clear of involving himself in such matters. But as he was currently the only adult Kringle in town, it fell to him by default.

Tired of tossing and turning, he arose early and went downstairs to Martin's office. He'd procrastinated doing the research on the reporter for a couple of days, but the uncertainty that she brought loomed heavy in his heart, and it was time to figure things out.

Not wanting to wake Nora, he used the flashlight on his phone and crept quietly down to Martin's office. With the door shut, he flicked on the lights. Martin's office was warm and inviting, yet so different from their grandfather's office, where all the cousins had spent hours together while growing up. While their grandfather's office was a nod to the past with his large wooden desk, typewriter, and bookcase full of leather-bound tomes, Martin's was the poster child of modern rustic.

Jack approached the sleek minimalist desk made of reclaimed wood with cast-iron legs and sat in the ergonomic chair. Martin's desk was devoid of clutter save a potted plant, his laptop, and a picture of Sadie and Nora. The hardwood floor was softened by a large, textured rug with a geometric pattern, and on the wall hung black and white photos of all the Kringle workshops across the globe. His cousin was such a traditionalist that Martin's office surprised Jack. Still, the sense of family history was felt as strongly as in his grandfather's cluttered space. Jack mused that if he ever remained in one place long enough for an office, he'd want it like this one.

But now was not the time for contemplation. He opened Martin's laptop and entered the password written on a notepad beside the computer. "Let's see what we can find out about you, Miss Reporter," Jack muttered. He opened his phone and squinted at the picture he'd taken of the reporter's card from the drawer in the candy store. He typed in "Ava Mitchell reporter." As search results populated the screen, a sense of determination settled within him. He needed to figure out whether or not she posed a genuine threat.

It turned out there were several Ava Mitchells, but diving deeper into the search results, he found the right one. His eyes scanned the headlines, searching for any information that would help him unravel Ava's intentions. There were articles she had written and biographical information, but the worst that Jack could find out was that she'd been fired from her last position for misuse of resources, although no details were given.

If she wasn't working for anyone currently, why was she in Mistletoe? "There must be something I'm missing." Jack's fingers flew across the keyboard. He typed in Kringle family and connections and Ava Mitchell. Those keywords led him to some forum discussions, and then he found what he was searching for. The piece of the puzzle that made her interest in Mistletoe make sense.

Deep in the digital world was a forum entitled Santa Proof. He spent the next hour down that rabbit hole, discovering inaccurate and some surprisingly accurate representations of his family. One that stood out was from Ava Mitchell herself. According to Ava, her grandfather had worked for the Kringle family decades ago, and during his recent decline with dementia, he mentioned working for the Santa Claus family. At first, Ava thought it to be nonsense, but now she was determined to prove that he was, in fact, telling the truth. Unfortunately, Ava never mentioned her grandfather's name.

Some forum participants told her to leave well enough alone. Others shared her enthusiasm at uncovering the Santa secret.

Could this be true? Could her grandfather have worked for the Kringles? He continued his search and stumbled upon a small-town newspaper's online archive. There was a black-and-white photo of an older gentleman standing with a young girl in an industrial kitchen. Jack squinted at the accompanying article, trying to make out the faded text. The headline read "Grandpa Joe: The unsung hero of Pine Falls." The article described a very generous man who spent the weeks up to Christmas raising money to provide free Christmas dinner to all those in their town and surrounding area who wanted it. The young girl in the picture was his granddaughter, Ava Mitchell. Nothing about the text indicated he was angry or bitter, longing to reveal the Kringle family secret. In fact, he embodied the holiday spirit. Surely, he had no vendetta against them, so what was Ava trying to prove?

Jack noted his name on a pad of paper and checked the time on his phone. In a couple of hours, he'd call Ellie and have her search for the man's name in the archives. Even if Joe Mitchell once worked for the Kringles, what could Ava gain from revealing their secret and thus destroying generations of tradition and Christmas magic? "Think, Jack, think," he urged himself, tapping the pen against his lips. "What would drive her to come after us now? What's her angle?" The questions swirled around in his head, each one adding another layer of complexity to the puzzle before him.

If only I could talk to Rosie. The thought surprised him as he had grown accustomed to handling things himself. But more than surprise, this caused the gravity of the situation to hit him like a freight train: not only did he have to protect his family legacy, but their situation required him to ensure the safety and happiness of all those who worked for them, the entire town of Mistletoe, the Snowflake Sugar Shop, and a red-headed candymaker named Rosie Plum.

·♥·♥·♥·♥·♥·

Jack arrived at the Snowflake Sugar Shop to find Rosie behind the counter, absentmindedly rearranging candy jars. Her usually bright green eyes were clouded with worry, and her fingers trembled slightly as they gripped a jar of pink and white striped peppermint sticks. He thought he'd helped her relax and rediscover the joy of both winter and candy making. But something was clearly bothering her.

He approached her with a warm smile. "Hey there, Rosie," he said gently. "You look like you could use a break."

"I'm all right," she said, giving him a weak smile. "There's just a lot on my mind."

"Like what? I'm all ears."

Rosie sighed. "Well. First, I'm still trying to figure out what to do with 100 lbs of Isomalt. Second, I caught that reporter trying to dig up more dirt on Sadie and Martin. She was asking odd questions to Mayor Evergreen and Eleanor Frost. Luckily, when the mayor found out she wasn't with any magazine or news outlet, he stopped talking and told her to make an appointment. Something about the situation has me on edge. It's like she's up to something nefarious."

Jack's body tensed. He was at a loss for words when what he originally planned to do was comfort Rosie.

She glided around the counter, her movements as fluid and enticing as molten chocolate. As she delicately placed her hand upon his arm, a wave of warmth cascaded through him, stirring his senses. Her simple touch, tender and soothing, enveloped him in a sensation so intense it was as if she had caressed his soul with a brush of decadent, velvety chocolate fondue.

He swallowed hard.

"Your idea of a break might be exactly what I need. I'm going to step out for a moment. I'm going to the post office to drop off a couple of online orders and grab some coffee. Do you want anything?"

"Sure, I'll take a black coffee, no sugar." Jack hoped he sounded normal and nonchalant.

"Alright, be back in a minute," she said, giving him a small smile before slipping out the door, leaving Jack alone.

Jack wiped at the thin layer of perspiration on his brow. How odd. He never sweat. His body ran cold, and he preferred it that way. The stress of the reporter, and yes, the physical effect Rosie had on him, were definitely taking their toll—a sensation he wasn't particularly familiar with.

Guilt about the reporter poking around weighed him down. News of the truth would destroy Mistletoe and, along with it, Rosie's store. He had to do something, but first, he wanted to see the smile return to Rosie's face. His eyes settled on the large front window, and an idea formed. Determined to lift her spirits, as he'd done by taking her skating, Jack went into the kitchen for supplies. While the Isomalt was melting, he shaved some white chocolate. When everything was ready, he carried his supplies to the front window.

With a deep breath, Jack began to work on his creation. Using the Isomalt and a brush as a rouse to hide his magic, his hands moved deftly over the glass as he built up layers of intricate frost patterns. He had always been skilled at crafting delicate designs, but this time, it felt different—as if each stroke of his fingers held more meaning, fueled by his desire to cheer up Rosie.

Each swirl and flourish danced across the glass, weaving together to create a breathtaking winter scene of snowflakes and icy branches. It was as if Jack had captured the essence of their day skating together and trapped it within the confines of the shop window.

He paused to examine his work. It still lacked something—a sense of movement. With a gentle wave of his hand, Jack summoned more magic and infused it into the frost scene. Delicate ice crystals glittered and danced with an ethereal light, casting a mesmerizing spell upon anyone who gazed upon the window display. The frost branches seemed to sway gently in an invisible breeze while the snowflakes sparkled like tiny diamonds caught in a moonlit dance. The entire scene was imbued with an otherworldly beauty that could only be achieved by the touch of Jack himself.

Had he gone too far?

The door opened, and a tall woman with dark hair stepped inside. Jack's chest tightened, recognizing her from his research. This was Ava Mitchell. He silently urged himself not to panic.

"Wha-what is this?" she stammered, struggling to tear her gaze away from the window.

"That is my latest creation," Jack said as casually as he could, putting all his energy into maintaining a carefree demeanor. "We're working on something special for Valentine's Day."

"Special? This is more than special, and that means you must be Jack Kringle. My sources told me another Kringle cousin was in town."

Jack's stomach dropped to his feet. What had he done? Had she seen the entire thing? "Your sources?" he scoffed. "Everyone knows everything in this town, and I am no great mystery." He walked over and held out his hand. "And you are..." He hoped he didn't sound as alarmed as he felt.

The reporter looked at his hand, as if nervous, before taking it and shaking. "Ava Mitchell."

"Nice to meet you, Ava. What brings you to Mistletoe so that you require sources?"

"I'm researching the town," she began, and then Jack witnessed her face change from confusion to anger. "And you're just the person I'm looking for." She glanced at the window, then back to Jack. "I know who you are, who your family is."

"Everyone knows my family around here."

"That's not what I mean, and you know it." She stepped toward him, pulled out her phone, and took pictures of the window display. "How did you manage to create such a lifelike scene out of frost?"

Before Jack could answer, Rosie's voice came from behind. "Frost? Come on, Ms. Mitchell. Don't be so ridiculous. But if you really must know our secrets, I accidentally ordered too much Isomalt, and we are thinking up creative ways to use it while promoting our store for Valentine's Day."

Jack nodded and pointed to the tub of Isomalt.

Ava turned toward the Isomalt then glared at Rosie, "You can't tell me that—"

Rosie cut her off. "I believe I told you the other day that if you're not going to buy anything, then you need to leave the store, and I'd appreciate it if you stop harassing my employee."

"Your employee?"

"Yes. Jack is a chocolatier, and we hired him for the month. Now, if you don't mind, we have a lot of work to do to prepare for Valentine's Day."

Ava Mitchell's gaze flickered between Jack and Rosie. The air crackled with tension as she locked eyes with each of them, a silent storm brewing in the depths of her stare. "This isn't over," she said, her voice low and resolute. With a swirl of determination, she turned on her heel and stormed out of the store, the door slamming behind her like the final note of a symphony, leaving a palpable sense of unrest hanging in the air.

Jack sighed with relief, but that ended the second he glanced at Rosie and saw her tight, angry expression, a line of concern etched between her eyebrows. Two coffees were on the counter before her—she'd returned to the store via the back door. How long had she been standing there, and how much had she seen?

"You better start talking," she said.

He'd been caught using magic. Now, he didn't know what to do. He truly believed he could trust Rosie, but his secret hung heavy in the air, pressing down on him. Could he really share his truth with her? And if yes, was it fair to burden her with such knowledge?

Chapter 10

ROSIE'S GAZE LOCKED ONTO Jack, her body rigid and unyielding. She remained still, like a deer caught in the unrelenting glare of oncoming headlights. A whirlwind of questions stormed through her mind, each echoing the same bewildering inquiry: What had she just witnessed? The room closed around her, the air thickening with tension. Suddenly, a wave of heat overcame her, breaking through her frozen state. She felt beads of sweat forming on her forehead, a stark contrast to the chill that had gripped her only moments before. With trembling hands, she hastily stripped off her winter wear, her movements mechanical and disjointed. She hung her coat on the hook with a sense of finality, as if shedding not only her clothes but also a layer of armor, leaving her feeling exposed in the aftermath.

"Rosie, please, don't be afraid of me." Jack's voice was a soft entreaty, filled with a vulnerability that contrasted sharply with the strength she usually saw in him.

"I'm not," Rosie said, but her words faltered, unconvincing, even to her own ears.

"Your hands. They're shaking." Jack took a cautious step toward her as if afraid to startle her.

Instinctively, Rosie retreated a step, her back stiffening. She couldn't deny the fear nipping at her heart. "What do you expect after what I witnessed?" she countered, her voice laced with a mixture of fear and disbelief.

Jack's expression turned earnest. "I know, but we need to act normal, especially if that reporter is lurking around." His eyes scanned the area, a hint of wariness clouding his features.

"Normal?" Rosie's laugh was bitter, tinged with incredulity. "How can I—" She broke off, her resolve crumbling. "I'm going to the back."

Jack followed her, maintaining a respectful distance. The air between them was charged with tension, an invisible thread pulling taut with every step they took. "I don't even know where to start." His voice was low and strained and there was a raw honesty in his admission that touched Rosie.

She closed her eyes tightly, wishing for a momentary escape. If only she could open them to find herself safe in her bed, away from this complicated reality. But when her eyelids lifted, Jack's gaze, intense and filled with concern, met hers. "Start at the beginning, I guess," she murmured, resigning herself to the truth she was about to hear.

Jack's plea was almost desperate. "Promise me you won't think I'm crazy. Promise to listen without walking out." He ran a hand through his hair.

Rosie nodded a silent commitment. "I'll do my best," she said, her voice steady, signaling her readiness to face whatever truths lay ahead.

"Thank you. That means everything to me." He exhaled loudly, clearly steeling himself. "The Kringle family is—boy, this is harder than I thought so I'll just say it. We're part of a legendary magical family. In fact, as far as we know, our descendants go way, way back to the times of Vikings and beyond. During that time, the magic was more like mine." He swallowed. "I possess the powers of who you may know as Jack Frost. Others in my family have a different kind of magic."

The room fell so silent that Rosie thought she could hear the synapses in her brain firing. Magic. Jack Frost. That was utterly ridiculous—yet she'd stood in awe, watching Jack create that image on her window. No. It couldn't be real.

Rosie's patience snapped like a brittle twig. "Not funny, Jack," she said sharply, her hands finding their way to her hips in a gesture of frustration and disbelief. "You want my help with that prying reporter? Fine. But spinning these absurd tales about belonging to some magical family? That's cruel and childish."

Jack's face was a mask of earnestness, his eyes imploring her to understand. "I'm not joking, Rosie, I swear," he insisted, the desperation in his voice was almost palpable.

Rosie shook her head, her heart racing with confusion and disbelief. "This is too much, Jack. Too far-fetched, even for you. Next, you're going to tell me that Eleanor Frost is—"

"No. Rosie, please. I'm serious. And Eleanor's name is a mere coincidence. That's all. Believe me." Jack leaned in closer, his voice dropping to a serious tone. "You know I didn't create that image with Isomalt. You even covered for me with the reporter. Deep down, you know it's true. Let me prove it to you."

Rosie's breath hitched in her throat. The sincerity shining in Jack's eyes was like a beacon in the fog of her uncertainty, and against her better judgment, she found herself leaning toward belief, wanting to trust in the unbelievable. "Alright," she whispered. She was teetering on the edge of doubt and belief, unsure whether this was a step toward truth or folly.

He held out the palm of his hand and closed his eyes. Rosie watched, speechless, as a large snowflake materialized in his palm, each intricate branch shimmering under the overhead lights. Slowly, the delicate ice crystal began to dance and twirl as if caught in an invisible breeze. Jack opened his eyes, and the snowflake left his hand, swirling in the distance between them, before landing on Rosie's cheek, sending a shiver down her spine. It was as if winter itself had given her a gentle kiss.

Her knees trembled, and she thought she might pass out. Suddenly, Jack was supporting her, guiding her over to a stool. "How did you do that?"

"Magic," he answered simply.

"I don't know what to say. Or think," Rosie said in a shaky voice. "This is all so...unbelievable."

"Take your time," Jack reassured her. His hand reached out and covered hers.

His hand was icy, yet the gesture warm.

Suddenly, the door chimed, and several boisterous customers entered the store. "Stay here," Jack said. "I got this."

Rosie nodded as if in a trance. With Jack out of the room, she rubbed at her temples. If everything Jack was saying was true, then everything she understood about the world had shifted. If he was lying, then she was falling for the biggest con job in history. She didn't know which was worse.

Finally, Jack returned.

"Maybe we should close for the day," she said. "I don't know if I can think, let alone work."

"I know it is a lot to process, and you need space to think things through, but we can't close the store." His voice was somber. "I screwed up. Really, really screwed up. And now the reporter is on to me. If we close, she'll think we have something to hide. I can't take that chance. I need to protect my family."

Rosie found herself at a loss for words. But as she looked into Jack's eyes, she realized that he'd offered her not only proof but trust—trust that she would keep a secret for both him and his family. She nodded. "You're right. We'll keep the store open, but I'm going to stay back here if that's okay with you."

"Anything you want," he said.

The afternoon kept Jack busy. His handiwork on the window had garnered quite a lot of attention, making it the most bustling day since his arrival. Despite the hive of activity upfront, Rosie remained secluded in the back, engrossed in her own world. Throughout the afternoon, Jack found himself peering into the backroom, concerned. Each time, he found Rosie meticulously reorganizing shelves and rearranging candy jars, her movements deliberate yet distant. She purposely avoided meeting his gaze, choosing instead to immerse herself in mundane tasks, her demeanor a mix of determination and evasion.

Jack's repeated attempts to engage her in the day's activity were met with silent resistance. Her reluctance to join him out front, to bask in the day's success, weighed heavily on him.

As the day waned and the Alaskan twilight cast a soft glow over the candy store, Jack's fatigue became palpable. The mental strain of worrying about Rosie, his screwup in front of the reporter, and the physical demands of managing the busy store single-handedly left him drained. With a deep sigh, he approached the front door. His fingers hesitated momentarily before he flipped the sign from 'Open' to 'Closed,' signaling the end of a day as rewarding as it was taxing.

"Okay, I'm off," said Rosie.

"Wait, Rosie," Jack pleaded. "We need to talk."

Rosie sighed. "I need rest. My entire world has been turned upside down."

"I understand, but please let me explain everything. Have dinner with me at Martin's cabin. I want you to understand everything about my family."

The distant glaze in her eyes vanished, replaced by a sharp, keen awareness. What had he said to cause such a transformation?

"Of course," Rosie said. "Your family. Including Sadie, Nora, and Martin. That means Sadie knows, too."

"Yes," Jack exclaimed, wanting to seize the opening he had to help Rosie's tension ease. "Martin told her everything. And just like you, it took her a while to understand and accept this new reality. So please, come for dinner, and I'll tell you everything. I promise." He held out his hand.

She paused briefly, then delicately placed her hand in his, causing his heart to race. Her slender fingers, skilled in crafting confections and bearing faint scars from hot sugar burns, felt surprisingly cold against his perennially chilly hands. He yearned to infuse them with warmth, to share the fire that ignited within him whenever he made contact with her. Yet, he recognized that there was so much more to her touch than physical attraction; it symbolized trust, the most precious gift of all.

Chapter 11

T HE SLEIGH SLOWED TO a gentle stop outside Martin and Sadie's cabin, the elk's breath misting in the cold air. Rosie reluctantly pulled her gaze away from the enchanting snowfall, nerves bubbling up inside her for the dinner invitation. "Are you doing this? Are you making it snow?"

"No. I don't control the weather. I don't have that kind of power. But please come in, and I'll explain everything."

As they approached the front door, the warm glow from the windows beckoned them inside. Jack swung the door open, revealing a cozy log cabin filled with laughter and the tantalizing aroma of a home-cooked meal.

"Rosie!" Nora exclaimed, rushing forward to envelop her in a hug. "Jack texted that you were coming. I'm so glad."

"Thanks," Rosie said, returning the embrace, realizing again that someone she knew and cared about lived in a magical world.

"Ellie really outdid herself tonight," Nora added. "You've met Ellie, right?"

"Yes, I've met her a few times now."

"Let's go into the kitchen, shall we?" suggested Jack.

Rosie nodded, following him into a large room with modern appliances made to look vintage, cupboards flanking the walls, and a large kitchen island with a concrete top. A fire crackled in the corner across from a live-edge dining table and sectional sofa. The open-concept room was clearly the hub of the home, and a pang of longing for her childhood home washed through her.

"Why hello, Rosie, have a seat at the island and help yourself to some snacks. Dinner will be ready in a few minutes," Ellie said.

Rosie smiled and followed Ellie's instructions. She assumed Ellie was Martin's business assistant, not a servant.

"Ellie doesn't normally make us dinner," Jack said as if reading her mind. Oh goodness, could he do that?

"How did you know I wondered that?" she asked him.

He laughed. "I'm not a mind reader. Just making friendly conversation. Ellie and I grew up together, so she likes to spoil me when I'm in town."

"You mean I like to make sure Nora is eating a variety of food groups," Ellie replied.

"I cook. We had fruit last night."

"Chocolate-dipped strawberries don't count," Ellie chastised Jack. The familial banter of long-time friends warmed Rosie, making her miss the casual warmth of the family dinners of her youth. What would her parents do if they knew what she did?

Nora walked over to the sink and poured herself a glass of water. "So, how did Uncle Jack convince you to come for dinner?"

"Oh, um," Rosie struggled and turned to Jack sitting beside her.

"Yeah. We need to talk about that. Basically, I used my magic on the window in the candy store and didn't realize Rosie was behind me." Jack ran a hand over his face. "I also didn't see the reporter."

Rosie watched Nora's and Ellie's eyes open wide.

"Oh, Jack." Ellie's hand covered her mouth, and the room filled with a silent, palpable tension.

"I won't tell anyone, I swear," Rosie said.

"Oh no, Rosie, honey," Ellie said. "That's not the issue. We know Sadie trusts you, and that's enough for us. The problem is the reporter. She's out to reveal our secret."

"That's right," Nora said. "As Sadie always says, you're Snowflake Sugar family. Now, you're more than that. You're honorary Kringle family."

Rosie's eyes teared up. "Thank you. This is a lot to digest. I'm grateful you're not mad that I found out."

"If they're mad at anyone, it will be me. And completely justified. My use of magic out in the open was reckless. I know better than that."

"What did you do?" asked Ellie.

"I created a picture out of frost on the window."

"Why?" Nora asked.

Jack gave them a sheepish grin. "I was trying to cheer up Rosie."

"You what?" Rosie snapped.

Jack shrugged. "You were so tense. I thought a picture celebrating winter and the time we went skating would help."

Wow. He'd taken such an enormous risk for her. Rosie's heart beat faster. "Thank you," she whispered. "I'm sorry it got you into trouble."

"Now, what do we do?" asked Nora.

"Actually, without even knowing the reality of the situation, Rosie told Ava Mitchell that I was using up the Isomalt she'd ordered too much of."

"It helped that he had a bowl of Isomalt beside him. I think she believed it. After all, it's easier to believe than the truth," Rosie said.

"And that should buy us some time, but I did some research on Ava Mitchell, and I can't figure out what she is trying to do—I mean, yes, she is trying to expose our family, but I don't understand why. Her grandfather used to work for the Kringles and, from what I can tell, was a kind and generous man. There are no articles about him trying to convince people that the Kringles are magical."

Ellie smiled at Rosie. "This is all a bit much, my dear, isn't it? Not only do you learn about the Kringle magic, you are embroiled in a situation that can threaten us all. Not a good way to welcome you into our circle, is it?"

"It's a lot for sure, and to be honest, I'll probably lie awake all night, but Sadie is my best friend, and I've come to know Martin and Nora quite well—although not as well as I thought." She attempted to laugh.

"I get it. It's not every day you find out about magic and that Santa Claus is real," Nora said.

Rosie jumped off her stool. "What?"

Jack cringed. "I was building up to that, Nora."

Breathing became labored, and Rosie was certain she was going to pass out.

Ellie rushed over. "Sit down," she said, guiding Rosie to the couch. Rosie leaned forward, her head in her hands.

Jack passed her a paper bag. "You're hyperventilating. Here. Breathe into this."

Rosie did as she was told. Her head spinning. She was dreaming. She had to be. But pieces began to click into place. Martin's toy store and factory, the sleigh. Oh goodness, their last name was Kringle. Mistletoe was a real Santa Village. Of course, of course, of course. It was all as real as the smell of dinner cooking, the fire crackling, and the comfort of Jack's hand on her back. If Sadie could handle this, so too could she. What choice did she have?

Rosie calmed her breathing and leaned back. "Sorry. That last revelation was more than I was expecting."

"I'm sorry," Nora said.

"It's okay. I shouldn't have been that shocked, what with the toy factory and all. It's—wow. Can I have a glass of water, please?"

"Of course." Ellie returned with a cool tumbler of water and handed it to Rosie.

She held it to her forehead, then drank it down.

"It's not that complicated," Jack said. "I told you the magic is old, and it is. But over time, things evolved as they often do. No one knows for sure what came first, Santa magic or the idea of Santa, but our family took on the role of Santa, delivering joy and cheer to the world." He scratched his chin.

"I can't believe Sadie married Santa Claus. Oh," Rosie's hand covered her mouth. "She's Mrs. Claus."

Jack gave her an odd look.

"There's more, isn't there?" Rosie asked.

"Yes," Nora said. "My dad is *a* Santa, not *the* Santa."

"Sorry, what?"

"Think of it like this," Jack said. "Imagine that the Kringles manage an international toy-making business. We have a CEO who is my grandfather, two vice presidents, my mother, and Martin's father, and then there are eight Santas spread across the globe. They are my cousins, but not everyone in the family becomes a Santa. Some prefer other roles in the business, and then some Kringles are born a little different, with more ancient powers, like me."

"You could be a Santa if you wanted to, Jack," Ellie said.

"I know, but my passion lies elsewhere." Jack turned from Ellie and smiled at Rosie. "Are you hanging in there?"

"So far."

"Good, so, before you ask, no, we don't have elves. The people who work for us are regular people like you and Sadie—like Ava Mitchell's grandfather. They just happen to work for a magical family. Usually, we keep our villages hidden, but something went wrong in Mistletoe, and the only way we could access our power source was to move into town or pack up and find a new location. Martin had fallen for Sadie by that point, so when Sadie and Nora came up with the idea of hiding in plain sight...well, the rest is history. Except that now, my carelessness has put us all at risk.

"That reporter was already snooping around, Jack. It's not your fault," Ellie insisted.

"That's nice of you to say, but it is, and now I need to do something about it. I just don't know what."

"Let's put that aside for a moment and enjoy dinner," Ellie said. "I can't think on an empty stomach. Nora, come help me set the table."

Rosie watched Nora and Ellie go to the cupboards to gather plates and silverware. She'd never experienced a migraine before, but she wondered if she was getting one then. Her head throbbed.

"You're sure you're okay?" Jack asked.

"Honestly, I don't know. But thank you for trusting me with all this. I'm sure it's not easy to tell people your secret."

"I've never told anyone before," Jack admitted. "But you shouldn't be thanking me, as carrying this secret is also a burden."

Rosie's heart swelled with empathy and affection. "That's what friends are for," she said, her words more than a response—they were a promise. As Jack's hand accidentally brushed against hers, a surge of electricity shot through them, a tangible current of connection that was impossible to ignore.

Rosie turned to look at Jack and, in that moment, lost herself in the depth of his chocolaty brown eyes. It was as if time had stilled, the world around them fading into a blur. In his eyes, she saw not only the man who held a secret but the soul of someone who had bravely shared his true self. Her heart skipped a beat, recognizing the unspoken bond forming between them—deeper and more profound than friendship.

"Dinner!" Nora called out.

Startled, Rosie nodded.

"Coming," called Jack, standing and extending his hand for Rosie. She took it with no hesitation.

"Rosie," Jack said softly, his voice barely audible over the clink of silverware and plates. "I want you to know... I'm happy you're here."

"Me too, Jack." Rosie's heart skipped a beat. "More than you know.

·♥·♥·♥·♥·♥·

Rosie stared at the ceiling all night. Her world had changed so fast. People she cared about were magical. Santa Claus was real. Jack had the power of Jack Frost. Unable to lie in the silence any longer, she called out to her virtual AI assistant. "Tell me about the history of Jack Frost."

"Here is a summary of Jack Frost," the computer voice said.

Jack Frost is a popular figure in folklore and mythology, primarily associated with cold winter weather. His origins are somewhat unclear, as he embodies characteristics from various cultural traditions.

In many European cultures, Jack Frost is seen as a mischievous spirit responsible for frosty weather, nipping at noses and toes in the cold, and painting intricate frost patterns on windows during winter. His character is often portrayed as playful yet biting, symbolizing the harshness of winter.

The name "Jack Frost" seems to be of British origin, but similar figures can be found in other cultures. For example, in Russia, he is known as

Morozko or Father Frost, a more benevolent figure who gifts children with presents in winter. In Norse mythology, there's Jokul Frosti, or "Icicle Frost," believed to be one of the sons of Kari, the Norse personification of the wind. This connection ties Jack Frost more closely to ancient mythologies, depicting him as a powerful natural force. However, it's important to note that the Norse legends don't personify winter or frost in quite the same whimsical or benign way as the later folklore surrounding Jack Frost. Norse myths often depict their frost giants as formidable and sometimes threatening figures, embodying the harsh and dangerous aspects of winter and the natural world.

In American and Canadian cultures, Jack Frost is a popular figure in literature and media, often depicted as a sprite-like character with icy powers. He's been the subject of various poems, movies, and songs, evolving into a symbol of winter's magic and whimsy. This portrayal has made him an enduring character in winter holiday traditions, where he's often featured alongside other winter figures like Santa Claus and the Snowman.

Overall, Jack Frost remains an embodiment of winter's chill, a blend of various cultural traditions and stories. His evolution from a mischievous sprite to a more rounded character in modern media reflects the enduring human fascina-

tion with winter and its whimsical,
yet harsh, beauty.

So, Jack's history consisted of legend. His genealogy stemmed from Norse gods and European mythology. He was a living, breathing figure from folklore, yet he worked at the candy store making chocolate confections. He was a human being who made a snowflake appear out of nowhere in the palm of his hand and created a stunning image out of frost in her storefront window.

And she liked him.

Not only did she find him attractive, but Jack had proven himself hardworking and thoughtful. He challenged her and sometimes drove her mad, but she'd needed a bit of a shake-up. And under his arrogance, he was kind. He'd taken her skating to the most beautiful—wait. Had Jack done that? Created a perfect place just for her?

Holy moly.

The coffee maker turning on was her cue that morning had arrived, so she rose from her bed and stepped into the shower. She could walk around in this foggy stupor and be useless, or she could help Jack—the man who made a winter paradise specifically for her. Not only that, protecting his family's secret would also save the town she loved.

Her choice was an easy one.

Chapter 12

ROSIE STOOD IN THE middle of the candy store, as she often did these days. Things had changed so much recently that it didn't feel real. the Snowflake Sugar Shop had been her haven, then when she'd become co-owner, a place of stress, now it had become the epicenter of an unfolding fairy tale, with her, Rosie Plum, in the center of it all. Not to mention Jack Kringle, the chocolatier whose hands crafted more than confections.

She bit her lip, pondering her new reality and how life beheld mysteries beyond anything she ever imagined possible. This new world came wrapped in a tapestry woven with threads of wonder and anxiety. Her town thrummed with hidden magic. Her best friend was Mrs. Claus. Her temporary chocolatier held in his hand the enchantment of winter.

The door jingled, snapping her from her reverie. She saw Jack enter, noting the way his eyes found hers instantly. They sparkled with a familiar twinkle, reflecting relief. They stood in silent communion amidst the shelves laden with their confectionary wonders.

Rosie spoke first. "Well, if it isn't the man, the myth, the legend."

Jack laughed. "I wasn't sure if you'd make it into work today."

Rosie's shoulders lifted into a soft shrug. "I don't know how helpful I'll be today as I didn't sleep a wink, but you need to know I'm here for you...and your family. Last night's revelations jolted me like a shockwave, and I'm still grappling with everything, but know this: your family's legacy, our town, and yes, even you hold a special place in my heart. So, what we need to do is come up with a plan."

Before she could utter another word, Jack closed the distance between them, wrapping Rosie in a hug and pulling her tight against him. His embrace was a haven, the comfort of his touch seeping into her bones. His breath stirred her hair, carrying the faint scent of cocoa and warm spices. They fit together like two perfect truffles nestled in a velvet-lined box.

"Thank you so much," he whispered. "This means everything to me. I know I screwed up, and this is all my fault. So, thank you for accepting me, and thank you for helping."

In his arms, Rosie felt a surge of safety, a comforting assurance that, in his embrace, the world's chaos could be tamed. The store, the town's mysteries, and even her tumultuous heart seemed manageable. If only Jack wasn't leaving in a few weeks. His impending departure loomed over them, casting a shadow on the moment. Rosie, feeling a tear escape, gently stepped back. "We should start planning," she said, her voice steady despite the storm of emotions brewing within.

They retreated to the store's cozy back room, where Rosie booted up her laptop. Jack sat close, his presence a blend of comfort and distraction.

Rosie's voice wavered as she spoke. "Okay, so with sales down at this time of year, I originally planned to do something big on social media. People don't turn to a Christmas-themed town for things other than Christmas, but we can't wait for tourists to arrive again to make money. Aside from this magic issue, Snowflake Sugar needs to make money to survive. I can't have this store fail. I won't." She noted the rise in her voice and felt her heartbeat quicken at the thought of losing the store. Maybe it was due to her fragile emotional state brought on by the revelation of magic or her lack of sleep, but whatever caused it, her anxiety over losing the store reared its head, adding to her stress.

"I thought the store was doing well, financially," Jack said, his surprise clear.

"It's fine, but once you start down that slippery slope, sometimes there is no turning back. And it affects not only the business but every aspect of life. It's hard to recover from failure."

Jack swiveled his chair to face her, his expression earnest. "Okay. What's going on?"

"Nothing, nothing. I just don't want to fail."

"You're not failing. I realize you need to always focus on the bottom line, but there's more going on here."

Rosie closed her eyes. Why was this haunting her now? Was it her mind distracting her from the magic issue? And did she want to share her emotional baggage with Jack? When he placed his cool hand on her arm, her defenses crumbled. She opened her eyes and stared at the tabletop.

"My childhood was wonderful, and I thought I had the perfect family. My parents were kind and loving toward me and each other. They had a dream to open a bakery, and one day their dream came true. Our lives were wrapped in sweetness for about a decade—until it wasn't. There were a couple of lean months, and they assumed the tide would turn, but it never did. It worsened until, eventually, they went out of business, and we lost everything. It broke them. They argued all the time. They went from a loving couple to distant strangers. We had to leave our house and move into a small apartment in another town. Things were never the same. I don't want to fail like that and lose my friends and community. Mistletoe is all I have." Rosie sighed, then continued, remembering how Mayor Evergreen and Eleanor Frost had questioned her ability to manage the store. "It sounds silly, but even though they failed, I seek their advice in my head. Perhaps I never should have agreed to become a partner. I was so happy simply making candy. Forget personal growth and all that. Forget career ambition. What if I can't do it and the business fails?"

The room fell into such a heavy silence that Rosie thought she might suffocate.

"I don't know what to say," Jack finally said. "I don't want to fill the air with platitudes. Sometimes, businesses fail. The reasons can be simple or complex. But your journey isn't defined by your parents' struggles. You can't surrender to fear before you've even begun to fight." He squeezed her arm. "I'm sorry to have complicated things. I've been cocky and arrogant since the day I arrived, and look where it's gotten us. My family and the entire town are at risk." He ran his hand through his hair. "My goodness, listen to me. I've made this problem about me when we were talking about you."

"Well, it is kind of your fault," Rosie teased, nudging him. Then she placed her hand on Jack's, wanting to support him as he had supported her because he'd changed her perspective in a few short sentences. The rapid shift in her outlook was so astonishing that it was a wonder she hadn't experienced whiplash. Her path wasn't defined yet—that one sentiment snapped her out of a funk she'd been in for months. She'd been so afraid of repeating her parents' mistake that she'd forgotten she was an active player in her own life. This gave her the burst of strength and courage she needed. Rosie gave Jack a quick squeeze and a kiss on the cheek. "Thank you. That was exactly what I needed to hear."

He raised an eyebrow. "That I've been arrogant and cocky?"

"Oh, I already knew that," she said playfully. "I'm referring to the part about giving up before even beginning to fight. Now, the way I see it, we can either mope around here or devise a plan to get Ava Mitchell off your back. Like I said before, I wanted to do something for social media. What if we do a live event? Then Ava Mitchell will have to wonder if we're using magic, right? Why would we expose your family's magic?"

"I don't understand. You're saying we should use magic?"

"Bear with me. I'm figuring this out as I go." She stood and poured herself a glass of water, drinking it all. "We make it appear to be magic and promote it as magic, but we don't use magic at all. Kind of like hiding in plain sight, like the toy factory, except that we won't be hiding anything. Does that make sense?"

"I think so. Keep going," Jack said.

And just like that, the creative juices that had been dammed now flowed freely. Rosie grabbed a piece of paper and began sketching, trying to conjure a spectacle that would merge the whimsy of Mistletoe with the charm of the Snowflake Sugar Shop. She scratched out one image, then moved on to the next. Eventually, a plan emerged, intricate and bold. She looked up, excited, and noticed she was alone. She wondered where Jack went until she heard him assisting a customer. She waited until the customer left, then jumped up, her heart full of newfound hope and determination.

"I've got it, Jack!" she exclaimed, her eyes alight with excitement.

·❤·❤·❤·❤·❤·

Jack faced Rosie, his heart warmed by her radiant smile. She was a vision of joy, her enthusiasm infectious. "What's the plan?"

Jack grinned as Rosie looked around the store as if there were spies.

"We're going to do this outside. Now, some of this depends on what the Kringle workshop can make us, but I'm assuming your people can create a track we can use under a layer of ice. What comes to mind is one of those miniature villages that people set up for Christmas, and you have an ice rink and figures moving around a track. Do you know what I mean?"

"Yes, and I'm pretty sure we can do that."

"Great. So because I have all that Isomalt, we're going to build a snowman and a snow-woman out of Isomalt, white chocolate, and other goodies. They will be on opposite sides of a small skating rink and then glide toward one another by the mechanics underneath the ice. Got it so far?"

"Yes."

"Okay, good. Now imagine some romantic music playing as they move toward the center, where they'll meet under an arch of red Isomalt hearts. Hidden inside the arch will be powdered sugar. When the snowcouple arrives, a fan will blow out the sugar, creating snowflakes, as in our name Snowflake Sugar."

Jack fell silent, awestruck. The plan was ambitious yet utterly feasible. "This is brilliant, Rosie. The sugar effect is pure genius."

Rosie took a stage bow, her laughter echoing in the store. "That's why they pay me the big bucks. Oh, wait, I pay me. But seriously, the key is to make the snowman and snowwoman look like they're moving by magic. The question is where and how."

Jack gazed out at the town square and scratched under his chin. He watched as a group of kids made their way toward the skating rink, and an idea began forming. "How about this? We propose to the mayor that we build a small skating rink for a Valentine's Day celebration, but since we want it to be a surprise, we ask that it appears to be a town works project—like a burst water main. Hopefully, that will keep Ava Mitchell away. Then, I'll get a team from the factory to create the infrastructure we need. From what Martin has told me about the mayor, he is very keen on any project that brings publicity to Mistletoe."

"You're absolutely right. I think that will work. And on the event day, we'll ensure Ms. Mitchell knows all about it. Oh, and I almost forgot. I would like you to make a few signs to go up around town—similar to the stunning picture on the window. That way, she knows we're not hiding anything. This is going to be amazing," Rosie said, clapping her hands.

"Thank you, Rosie. Your support in this means the world to me." Jack's voice trembled slightly, betraying the depth of his emotion. He gazed into her eyes, a mixture of gratitude and vulnerability shimmering in his own. "I've spent so much of my life running from family traditions. My gift always set me apart and made me feel like a stranger in my own world. But it wasn't until I nearly shattered the Kringle legacy that I understood my family's true value. Not only to the world but to me."

Rosie's eyes held a warmth that made the chilly room glow. "I'm sorry you felt that way, Jack." Her voice was a gentle caress in the quiet room, and the sincerity in her words wrapped around him like a comforting embrace.

"It wasn't anything my family did. It was all on me. I felt...feel...so useless. An anomaly in a world of anomalies."

Rosie reached out, her hand lightly touching his arm. "But Jack, if it means anything, I cherish your uniqueness. There's nothing more enchanting than winter, and your gift is a celebration of everything the season represents. You're not just lucky; you're special."

Jack's heart swelled with a mixture of relief and newfound hope. Rosie's words were like a soothing balm, healing old wounds he didn't know he still carried. Nodding slowly, he felt a profound sense of peace settle within him. Her belief in him, in his gift, was a powerful affirmation. And to think, he almost hadn't made the journey to Mistletoe. Now, he couldn't imagine being anywhere else. In Rosie's presence, he found not only acceptance but a deep, resonating connection that he had longed for all his life.

He cleared his throat. "Did you want to come to dinner again tonight? We'll need to tell Nora and Ellie the plan. Plus, Ellie will be the one to arrange the construction with a team of engineers."

"I don't want to impose."

"Oh, you're not. Nora considers you an honorary family member."

He watched as Rosie's eyes filled with tears.

"What did I say?" he asked.

"Nothing. But now that both my parents are gone, I've missed being part of a family. It's silly. I'm sorry."

Slowly, he made his way to her side and gently took her hands in his. His heart ached at the thought of her pain, wishing he could take it all away and wrap her in happiness. "Rosie, we are the lucky ones to have you," he said, gazing into her eyes with intense emotion. The steady thud of his heartbeat matched the clock's ticking on the wall. Jack leaned in closer, longing to feel her soft lips against his own. Rosie's expression mirrored his own curiosity and desire. But as they were about to close the distance between them, the door chimed loudly, shattering their moment like a delicate snow globe hitting the floor.

Chapter 13

JACK STOOD AT THE sink, the sleeves of his festive red flannel shirt rolled up to his elbows, steam rising from the sink and fogging up the windows. The scent of dish soap mingled with the woodsy fragrance that lingered within the walls of Martin's home. He was almost meditative as he swirled the sudsy water, his hands mechanically finding each pot and pan needing scrubbing.

The past week had been so busy he'd let the general upkeep of the house take a back seat, but now that everything was set up and ready to go tomorrow, he needed to get caught up. Neither Sadie nor Martin would appreciate the mess upon their return.

But there was also a degree of quiet comfort in the task, allowing his mind to wander enough, but not too far from Martin's kitchen. It was a welcome lull after the whirlwind of preparing the Snowflake Sugar Shop's event, a project that had consumed every waking moment of the past week.

A soft shuffle broke the silence of the cabin, and Jack's gaze shifted from the window to the doorway where Nora appeared, a mischievous glint in her big, curious eyes.

"Hey, Uncle Jack," Nora said as she leaned against the doorframe. "Are you attempting to scrub through the bottom of that pot?"

A half-grin tugged at Jack's lips. "I need to make sure I can see my reflection at the bottom."

"Is that so?" she chirped, moving closer to perch on the counter beside him. "Or are you lost in thought, daydreaming about someone?"

His cheeks reddened slightly, a blush creeping up beneath his stubbled jaw. "And who would that be, Miss Nosy?"

"Oh, I don't know. Maybe a certain redhead who's captured your attention?"

"We're friends. That's all," he said, trying to sound nonchalant, while that near-kiss replayed in his mind. Nora's knowing smile told him she wasn't buying it.

"Uh-huh, friends don't look at each other the way you two do." Nora's grin widened. "I see how you watch her when she laughs or ties that apron around her waist."

"Observant, aren't we?"

"Even the snowmen outside have noticed," Nora teased, her laughter echoing gently off the wooden walls.

"Alright, alright," Jack conceded with an exaggerated sigh. "Let's say, hypothetically, I do fancy Rosie. It doesn't matter because I'm leaving as soon as your father and Sadie return."

Nora's face turned serious. "The heart wants what the heart wants. Even if that heart belongs to a wandering chocolatier."

Jack sighed. Could he really entertain the idea of staying? Of letting his heart settle in one place? "Thank you, Nora, for the unsolicited advice."

"Anytime, Uncle Jack. Anytime."

"And since you're here…" He tossed a tea towel at her. "I wasn't the only one dirtying dishes this week."

She hopped off the counter, her laughter echoing around them as she sashayed to the drying rack.

They worked in silence for several minutes, Jack lost in his thoughts. His gaze drifted to the frosted windowpane, where the silhouettes of snowflakes clung delicately against the glass. The ebb and flow of his past wanderlust now seemed distant, like a story from someone else's book. In its stead was this budding hope, this gentle pull toward a future he hadn't dared to imagine until now.

"Earth to Jack," Nora chimed.

"Sorry," Jack said. "I was thinking about the event tomorrow." Not exactly true, but he didn't want the conversation to focus on Rosie or his feelings again.

"I've been thinking about that too," Nora admitted. "And I've been following Ava Mitchell online and stuff."

"So, stalking her," Jack teased.

"Investigating," Nora insisted. "I think she's trying to relaunch her career by having this groundbreaking story. It's as simple as that."

"Huh. She was fired from her last job. That can't look good on her resume."

"Right. And I discovered that her career meant everything to her. She was doing well but became overconfident and did some stuff she shouldn't have. At least, that's what it seems like to me. I think she figured she'd either never get called out for it or that she was untouchable. I don't know why her ego was so big. Yes, she was clearly on her way up, but so were a bunch of others. Journalism is highly competitive."

"Hmm," Jack pondered. Maybe this reporter wasn't so different from himself. He'd gotten careless and was now trying to fix the mess he'd caused. Ava Mitchell, albeit in a more selfish way, was essentially doing the same thing. "So what do you think that means?"

Nora shrugged. "I think it means that if she can't prove that our family is magical, she'll leave us alone and try to find another story. She's grasping at straws here, and I doubt she wants to have a discredited story hanging over her head."

"But she saw me use my magic."

"Did she? You and Rosie handled that well. And this thing tomorrow is about dispelling her belief, too, is it not?"

"It is."

"You know what else I was thinking?"

"I'm sure you're going to tell me."

"We make her feel welcome."

"Why should we do that?"

Nora rolled her eyes. "Because we're Kringles. You know, goodwill, joy, Christmas spirit, and all that. From what Ellie has discovered, everyone loved her grandfather when he worked for us. During that time, he won the Kringle Kindness Award three times. Once he left us, he received several awards for volunteering and community service. Maybe we can present her an award for her grandfather, like a Lifetime Community Spirit Award, or something like that. You know how the mayor loves pomp and ceremony. I'm sure he'd be on board with it."

Jack washed the last dish and handed it to Nora. He pondered everything she said and had to admit that the girl had a brilliant idea. After all, Rosie's support and kindness transformed how he viewed many things in his life. Perhaps a little kindness does go a long way.

"I think you're on to something," he said. "How old are you again?"

"You were born with the ability to manipulate ice and snow. I was born with the wisdom of the ages." Nora laughed and ran out of the room, dodging the dish sponge Jack threw at her.

He unplugged the sink, dried his hands, and pulled out his phone, hesitating before calling Ellie to discuss Nora's idea. Sitting down at the kitchen island, he rubbed his temples. He had a lot going on for someone who had always led a carefree lifestyle. He'd always resented family duty and expectations, but now he wanted to remain involved—and do so from Mistletoe. Jack dialed Ellie's number, ready to embrace the challenges that lay ahead for both his family and his heart.

Chapter 14

THE FROSTY AIR NIPPED at Rosie's cheeks as she stood beside the small skating pond, her breath forming delicate clouds that vanished into the twilight. Jack stood beside her, appearing almost as nervous as herself. He smiled when he caught her gaze. Rosie was happy the week had passed in a haze of work, work, and more work. Otherwise, she might have thought about that almost-kiss with Jack. No matter how much she liked him, getting involved with

Jack would be a bad idea. He was leaving, and Rosie couldn't handle the pain in her heart. She would miss him enough as it was, but if she acted on her feelings, that would make it a whole lot worse.

Rosie shivered with anticipation, her gloved hands clutching the edges of her warm coat. She knew that the Snowflake Sugar Shop had outdone themselves this year, creating a masterpiece that brought the entire town together for the Valentine's Day celebration. As Mayor Evergreen cleared his throat and adjusted his spectacles, Rosie's heart fluttered with excitement.

"Ladies and gentlemen," Mayor Evergreen began, his voice resonating through the crisp evening air, "we gather here today to celebrate not only the craftsmanship of the Snowflake Sugar Shop but also the unity and love that binds our community."

The crowd erupted in applause, their mittened hands clapping in unison. Rosie's eyes scanned their faces, taking in the joyous expressions illuminated by the soft glow of the surrounding lights. She couldn't help but smile; it was moments like these that made her grateful to live in such a close-knit town.

"As we unveil this year's Snowflake Sugar creation to kick off a weeklong Valentine's extravaganza involving all our town square businesses," Mayor Evergreen continued, "let us remember the power of love and friendship. Let us cherish the connections we've forged and appreciate the beauty of sharing special moments with one another."

Rosie's gaze shifted toward the crowd. There was Ava Mitchell, front and center, with her phone ready to film the event.

A comically large button sat before the mayor. As soon as the crowd counted down to three, he pressed the button and the fairy lights above the rink turned on. Jack reached over and squeezed Rosie's arm.

From either side of the rink, large red draperies were hoisted away, revealing two stunning figures in candy. On one side, a charming snowman, donned in an elegant top hat and a scarf, twinkled under the ambient lights, its body adorned with colorful candy buttons. Opposite, a snowwoman stands, equally mesmerizing, dressed in a delicate, shimmering gown made of candy, complete with a stylish hat and a matching scarf. Both are poised on the ice, looking as if they are ready for a romantic date.

Romantic music began playing on the town square speakers, and spotlights fell onto the snowman and snowwoman. Slowly and gracefully, they glided across the ice like enchanted beings before meeting in the center under a breathtaking centerpiece of intricately crafted Isomalt hearts. When their mitten-clad hands touched, a fan began within the arch, blowing the sugar snow onto the vignette, creating a dreamy atmosphere.

The crowd cheered. Then one little girl, who'd held out her tongue to catch snowflakes, squealed in delight. "It's snowing sugar." Soon, a cluster of children and a few adults near the front were all holding out their tongues. "It's snowflake sugar," someone cried.

Nora came running over, holding out her phone. "Look at all the likes and comments. We're a hit!" Then she ran off again and resumed her spot beside Ellie's son, who was posting the live event on social media.

"That was perfect!" Jack exclaimed, his eyes alight with excitement. "It couldn't have gone any better."

"It was as if they were really gliding," Rosie said in agreement.

"Can you believe this?" an elderly woman said, her eyes wide as saucers.

"It's stunning," another bystander agreed, his voice tinged with wonder.

"It's like a dream," a teenage girl sighed, leaning closer to the boy beside her.

Rosie could feel Jack's gaze on her, but she was too nervous to meet his eyes. Instead, she let herself bask in the collective enchantment, her own satisfaction mingling with the crowd's delight.

"How did they do that? The snow looks so real, it could be magic!" a voice rang out, punctuated by nods of agreement.

"Rosie, we've done it," Jack said softly, his voice barely carrying over the murmurs of admiration. "We've really done it."

She finally turned to him, her green eyes reflecting the fairy tale scene before them. "We have." This was more than sugar artistry; it was a piece of her heart, shared with the town that had become her family and the man standing beside her.

"Thank you, Jack," Rosie said. "For helping me bring this to life."

"It's I who should thank you, Rosie. Your creativity and optimism are inspiring."

The townsfolk continued to gasp and applaud, a resounding tribute to all the hard work and passion that Rosie and Jack had poured into every crystalline detail. But instead of enjoying the moment, all Rosie could think about was how stiff and formal her and Jack's conversations had become. They spoke as if associates, not people who'd worked side by side for days. Admittedly, they'd ignored the draw between them, what with Jack leaving and all. Rosie sighed. Perhaps it was for the best.

"Did you model these after anyone in particular?" an elderly woman asked, her eyes crinkled with delight as she peered closer at the snow-couple.

"Actually, they're inspired by the idea of timeless love," Rosie answered, tucking a stray curl behind her ear. They'd decided in advance, the type of answers they'd provide. "Love that moves and evolves, just like the figures skating toward each other."

Jack picked up where Rosie left off, his voice low and melodious. "And the mechanical aspect was a nod to my family's toy-making heritage. It's about blending tradition with innovation."

Rosie caught his eye for a moment, appreciation mingling with something deeper as they exchanged smiles. The townsfolk nodded, clearly impressed by the thoughtful integration of story and skill.

Before anyone could voice another question, a brisk tone cut through the murmurs of the crowd.

"A moment of your time?" Ava Mitchell had arrived, notepad in hand and a scrutinizing look in her eyes. Rosie felt a frisson of tension snake its way up her spine.

"Of course," Jack said coolly.

"Your display is quite the spectacle," the reporter started, her pencil poised. "But tell me, is there any truth to the rumors that real magic is involved? After all, the Kringle name does carry certain...implications."

Rosie held her breath, appreciating Jack's steadying presence beside her.

"Magic?" Jack chuckled, his relaxed stance belying the careful consideration behind his words. "Well, if by magic you mean long hours, meticulous planning, and a sprinkle of creativity, then yes, it's quite magical indeed."

The reporter's gaze sharpened, honing in on Rosie, who met her eyes unflinchingly. "You must admit, there's a certain mystique to your work."

"I was wondering myself, how do you get them to move so... fluidly?" An elderly man, his eyes twinkling with childlike wonder, gestured toward the skating figures.

Rosie cast a glance at Jack, whose hands were casually tucked into his pockets, a knowing smile on his lips. "Ah, Mr. Benson, it's all about balance, tracks, and very large magnets."

"Really, it's simple physics," Jack added, leaning forward to give their audience a conspiratorial wink. "A bit of momentum here, a careful pivot there, and voilà, they dance."

The reporter, notepad in hand, circled back to them, her heels clicking impatiently on the icy pavement. "But surely, there's more to it than science? The Kringle touch, perhaps?"

"Science can be quite magical in its own right," Rosie countered smoothly, her emerald eyes reflecting the soft twinkle of fairy lights strung above. "Wouldn't you agree, Jack?"

"Absolutely," he affirmed, his relaxed posture a silent testament to their shared confidence. "Chocolate tempering, sugar spinning—it might as well be alchemy to those not versed in the craft."

From the corner of her eye, Rosie watched as the reporter's cheeks pinked with frustration. It was clear she hungered for a whisper of enchantment that would sate her readers' appetite for mystique. But they would offer no such satisfaction.

The reporter huffed, scribbling something indecipherable before turning on her heel to approach a group of locals huddled near a steaming cocoa stand. Her questions floated through the crisp air, snippets of suspicion seeking cracks in their armor of normalcy.

"Is it truly just gears and glucose, or is there something more... otherworldly at play?" she asked a small group of people.

"Never seen anything like it, but Rosie and Jack are talented folks. Don't need no magic when you've got skill like that," Mr. Thompson, the barber, replied.

"Real magic?" A twinkle-eyed grandmother chuckled, shaking her head. "Child, the real magic is in allowing yourself to believe for a moment, even if your mind knows otherwise."

With each dismissal, the reporter's shoulders slumped incrementally, her quest for the fantastical meeting the unyielding wall of mundane truth. Rosie watched, her heart a symphony of relief and empathy. She understood the allure of an exposé to a reporter, especially when that information would change the world—and their career. But today, the charms of confectionery prowess and mechanical ingenuity prevailed, woven by their own hands, not by unseen mystical forces.

The crisp evening air buzzed with whispers and the soft crunch of snow underfoot as Mayor Gregory Evergreen's stately figure emerged from the throng of townspeople as he made his way back to the podium. "I have one last order of business before everyone moves off to take their selfies under the Mistletoe Love Arch. So, if you please, let's welcome our visiting chocolatier Jack Kringle up to the podium." Mayor Evergreen's voice cut through the pleasant chatter.

Jack nodded at Rosie before moving toward the podium. His gait was relaxed, even though his stomach was in knots. This could easily backfire.

"Thank you, Mayor Evergreen," Jack said, reaching the podium and turning to face the assembly. The microphone picked up the soft timbre of his voice, sending it rolling like a gentle tide over the sea of expectant faces. "I appreciate the warm welcome this town has given me, especially today, as we celebrate love and community."

He paused, his gaze scanning the crowd until it found the reporter—her notebook poised, her expression a blend of curiosity and purpose. Jack cleared his throat, his thoughts gathering like ingredients before being expertly blended into a speech.

"Today, though," he continued, his voice gaining strength, "I want to shine a light on someone who helped make the Kringle community, then his own neighborhood, a better place. A man whose legacy is as rich and enduring as the chocolate we shall enjoy tonight." He saw Ava lift her head a little higher, her pencil hovering in anticipation.

"Your grandfather, Ms. Mitchell," Jack addressed her directly now, "was more than a diligent worker for my family's business. He was a beacon of dedication and spirit for us all. It's not every day that we get to thank those pillars of our community, those who laid the foundations so that we could build upon them."

A few nods rippled through the crowd, a silent chorus of agreement.

"His contributions went beyond the walls of the Kringle toy business," Jack added, his hands gripping the sides of the podium in case they shook. "He dedicated himself to spreading joy and friendship, community and belonging, when he worked for the Kringles and when he left to pursue other interests."

In the quiet that followed, Jack felt the burden of history and the future resting on his shoulders. It was a new feeling for someone used to being unanchored, yet it grounded him in an unexpected way. He reached beneath the podium and lifted a polished mahogany plaque into view, its surface gleaming under the soft lights strung across the square. The crowd hushed, their collective breath forming plumes in the chilly air. "Can Ava Mitchell come to the stage, please?"

Jack watched as she wove her way through the crowd, her face stern and full of distrust. Finally, she stood beside Jack, her eyes narrow with skepticism.

The plaque was a testament to the old-world craftsmanship Kringles were known for. Intricate scrollwork framed a heartfelt inscription for Joe Mitchell. It read: "In honor of a man whose sweetness surpassed even the finest chocolate. His legacy is the joy and unity he brought to our community and beyond."

Ava Mitchell accepted the plaque, her fingers tracing the carved letters. "Thank you," she said softly, her voice barely louder than a murmur. "My grandfather always spoke highly of the Kringles." Then she fled the stage.

"Thank you, Jack," Mayor Evergreen announced. "And now it's time to get on with the festivities!"

The crowd applauded, and then a line began near the Love Arch so people could take pictures. Jack, Rosie, and Nora walked around with trays of candy samples, and Caleb set up a booth for hot chocolate and apple cider.

As the night wore down, the reporter approached Jack and Rosie.

"That was quite the homage to my grandfather," she said. "But you've got to admit, it's a little out of the blue."

Jack met the reporter's gaze squarely. "You can't blame us for researching who you are, Ms. Mitchell. You came into town determined to save your career by digging up dirt about my family and the town."

Ava's mouth fell open, but she couldn't argue with the truth.

"When we discovered who your grandfather was, it was my cousin's daughter who taught me a valuable lesson. You see, acts of kindness create a ripple effect, encouraging others to act compassionately, and contributing to a more harmonious society. It's easy to get caught up in the day-to-day and forget that. The Kringle community is devoted to promoting joy and goodwill, and your grandfather was an exemplary representation of that. It was only natural for us to pay our respects."

"So you think because you gave me a plaque, I'm going to stop researching my story?"

"You're missing the point," Rosie said. "It's about being kind for kindness' sake."

"Really? That's all this is?" She held up the plaque.

"Do I hope you don't pursue your mission to hurt my family and this town? Of course,"

Jack said. "But both of us know a plaque wouldn't stop that. I can't change your behavior, Ms. Mitchell. I can only control mine, and today I chose to be kind and appreciative. Your grandfather represented everything we Kringles stand for. Why not celebrate that instead of trying to destroy something he believed in?"

Ava Mitchell had no comeback. She simply stood there awkwardly before giving Jack a nod and walking away.

"Wow," Rosie said. "That was quite something."

Jack ran his hand through his hair and gave her a coy smile. "I wasn't making it up when I said Nora taught me a valuable lesson, you know. The world is pretty messed up and full of angry people. I can't change that. Nor can magic, but I can try to make my corner of it a better place."

"Oh my gosh, Uncle Jack," Nora said, having snuck up behind them. "Now you sound as corny as my father. What have I done?"

Rosie laughed.

Jack rolled his eyes and then joined in the laughter.

"Do you two want me to take your picture under the Love Arch?" Nora asked.

"Why would we do that? We've already got some great video for social media. We don't need anything else. Now if you'll excuse me, I'm going to say hi to Caleb."

Rosie walked away before Jack could protest. Embarrassment washed over him. He thought he'd feel many things tonight. Relief that the event was over. Satisfaction that it turned out well. Comforted by the knowledge that the lack of magic would cause Ava Mitchel to leave them alone. But now Jack drowned in embarrassment because Nora knew of his feelings for Rosie as he watched her leave.

"Dude, what are you doing, letting her walk away?" Nora asked.

"What am I supposed to do?"

"I don't know. You're the adult. Figure it out."

Jack sighed. "I'm not good at this kind of stuff. Besides, if she liked me, she'd have agreed to the photo."

"Maybe she's not sure how you feel."

"Well, I'm not sure how she feels."

"Oh, my goodness. You two are worse than my friends at school. You like her, tell her. What's the worst thing that can happen?"

My heart will get broken, Jack thought. But Nora was right. If she didn't want to pursue anything with him, he could pack up and leave as originally planned. But if she was interested in him, then what? Would he stay? Would that make him happy? Yes. Yes, it would.

"You're right, Nora. You're absolutely right."

"I don't know what you folks would do without me. Now I'm going to go hang out with my friends. I'll be back later."

Nora took off, and Jack scanned the crown for Rosie. The town square was busy and the line for the Love Arch was long. As much as he'd love to take her there, perhaps this wasn't the right venue. If he was going to tell her how much she meant to him, he wanted it to be special.

·♥·♥·♥·♥·♥·

Rosie never realized how good of an actress she was. She was smiling and laughing when, all the while, she wanted to run home. Tonight had gone better than planned. She knew without checking that their live event had gone well and that if their video didn't go viral, it would still do very well and orders would start coming in. Valentine's Day was still a week away, and they'd be busy. Which would be good, because that was the only way she could survive working with Jack. She longed for him to stay so they could explore their growing bond, but he was a self-proclaimed traveler. Why would he stay for her?

"Well, Rosie, you and Jack outdid yourselves. That was amazing," Caleb said.

"Thanks. I'm kind of relieved it's all over, though. It was a ton of work."

"I bet, and I'm glad my store had most of the parts you needed."

Rosie saw Ava Mitchell turn her head, obviously overhearing Caleb. If Jack's words hadn't changed her mind, hopefully, Caleb's comments sealed the deal.

Eleanor Frost approached where she and Caleb were talking.

"That was quite the display," Eleanor said. "You did good, you and Jack. You made the town proud." And with that, she walked away. Rosie and Caleb looked at one another in stunned silence. Finally, Rosie spoke. "Is it possible Jack's message about kindness having a ripple effect reached the heart of Eleanor Frost?"

"You might be right," Caleb said. "Where is Jack anyway?"

"Last I saw him, he was talking to Nora." She gazed in the direction where she'd left them, but neither was there anymore.

"Is it going to be strange when he's gone?" Caleb asked softly. "You've been joined at the hip for the past few weeks."

A blush crept up Rosie's cheeks. "We haven't been joined at the hip."

Caleb's chuckle was gentle, yet it held a note of teasing. "Well, you certainly seemed pretty cozy. I've been asked several times if there was something going on between you two."

"And you said what, exactly?"

He shrugged, his casual demeanor belying the protectiveness in his voice. "That it wasn't anyone's business."

"Thank you, Caleb. You're a good friend."

"You're welcome." He paused, leaning in slightly. "But now that it's just you and me, is there anything going on?"

Rosie hesitated, her heart aching with a truth she couldn't quite face. "He's leaving right after Valentine's Day, so no."

"That makes it sound like you wish he wasn't."

She gazed back at him, her emotions a tangled web. "Honestly, part of me does wish he were staying longer. But that part doesn't get a say in real life."

"Did you tell him how you feel?"

"No. Of course not. I'm not going to reveal my heart to a person who is leaving town. It's better this way."

He gave her a long look. "If you say so."

"I do," she said, yet as the words floated in the air between them, she couldn't deny the shadow of doubt and longing that clung to her heart. If she was so certain, why did she feel so bad?

Chapter 15

IT HAD BEEN ANOTHER grueling week at the candy store, and Jack was about to drop from exhaustion. Their event last week had caused sales to skyrocket, and Jack vowed it would be a long time before he made another heart-shaped truffle. Not to mention snow-couple candies in white chocolate. The palms of his hands ached from rolling so many balls. But now it was over, and Jack felt out of sorts.

Rosie walked over to the door and turned the store sign from 'Open' to 'Closed'. "Well, that was fun, but I'm glad it's over. I couldn't have done it without you." She gave him a smile. "So now that you're done here, where are you off to?"

"Trying to get rid of me already?" he asked teasingly, but he was trying to uncover her emotions. Would she miss him at all? He'd moved closer to where she stood, hoping the proximity would help him uncover her true feelings, but she dodged around him and went into the back, quickly returning with the broom. She began sweeping. "The faster we get cleaned up, the faster we can get out of here."

He sighed and began putting several items in the cooler and closing some display cabinets. Then he washed down all the counters and did the dishes.

Rosie walked in and checked her watch. "Looks like we did that in record time. I don't know how to thank you for your help. Since I don't know where you're going next, I couldn't get you a going away present, so I got you a gift card."

She pulled an envelope out of her pocket and passed it to him.

"What's this?"

"I told you, it's a gift card."

His heart dropped. After their intense weeks together, is that how Rosie planned to say good-bye? With a gift card? He accepted it, locking eyes with her. Her eyes, brimming with unshed tears, betrayed a storm of feelings she was un-willing to voice. He clung to that slender thread of hope. "Rosie—" he started.

"No. Stop," she interrupted, her hand raised in a plea for silence. "It's best if you leave now."

"But what if leaving is the last thing I want?" he protested gently.

"I'll be okay soon. Goodbyes just break me, that's all."

He raked his fingers through his hair, a ges-ture of frustration and longing. "I'm not talking about leaving this room, Rosie. You're missing everything I'm trying to say."

Her voice was a faint echo of confusion. "I don't understand."

"I know you don't," he said softly. "But please, come with me."

"Why? What's the reason?"

"Trust me, Rosie," he implored, turning to face her fully, his heart in his eyes. "There's something essential I need to show you, something only you can see."

The silence that enveloped the store was deafening, his heart throbbing the only sound in the void.

Rosie's voice was a mere whisper, fragile as glass. "I'm sorry. I can't."

His heart felt like it had been shattered. "Oh."

She stepped closer, her presence a bittersweet ache. "I like you, Jack. More than you can imagine. And I think you feel the same. But if I go with you tonight and it turns out I'm right, the pain of your departure will be unbearable."

Relief surged through him. A tidal wave of elation. Rosie didn't want him to go. "Rosie, you are the most brilliant, funny, and breathtaking woman I've ever known, but you're not so great at picking up on the subtext, are you?"

Her brows knitted in confusion. "What are you trying to say?"

Gently, he took her hands in his. "I'm saying that leaving Mistletoe is the last thing on my mind. Especially leaving you. I'm utterly head over heels for you."

Shock flickered in her eyes. "You don't want to leave? Really?"

He chuckled softly. "Why does that surprise you? We're a match made in heaven. We sync perfectly at work, share a love for winter's charm, and both have a deep passion for con fectionery...and we're equally inept at revealing our true feelings to the one we care about."

A laugh bubbled from Rosie, her smile out-shining the brightest stars. Jack couldn't resist any longer; he drew her in, and their lips met in a kiss that felt like the slow, tender unveiling of a precious gift. His fingers cradled her face tenderly, and as she melted into his touch, his heart swelled, threatening to overflow with happiness. The kiss deepened, each moment tasting of a future filled with hope, fervent passion, and the sweet, enduring flavor of love.

·❤·❤·❤·❤·❤·

Rosie was lost in a kiss that suspended time itself, each second hinting at endless sunsets and sugary moments yet to come. The reality that Jack was choosing to stay in Mistletoe, choosing her, Rosie Plum, felt more fantastical than any tale of magic. Excitement surged through her, joy flooding her heart, as a swarm of butterflies took flight in her stomach.

When they finally parted, their smiles mirrored each other in breadth and joy.

"I've been dying to ask you this all day," Jack began, a hint of nervousness in his voice. "Rosie Plum, would you be my Valentine?"

Rosie's response was immediate and exuberant. "Yes, yes!" She leaped into his arms.

"Thank goodness," Jack breathed out a sigh of relief. "I planned something special for tonight, a surprise. But you didn't want to come with me earlier..." He paused, a playful glint in his eyes. "Will you join me now?"

"Absolutely." Rosie's smile was uncontainable. "Should I bundle up?"

"What do you think?" he teased.

Her eyes sparkled. "And my skates?"

He gave a playful eye roll. "Of course. The whole idea was to charm you into being my Valentine."

She giggled. "And the magic?"

With a flourish, Jack waggled his fingers. "A touch of Jack Frost's magic might have been at play."

Drawn irresistibly back to him, Rosie nestled into Jack's embrace. "You don't need grand gestures," she whispered, her eyes locked with his. "Everything I've ever wanted is right here with you."

His reply was a soft echo of her sentiment. "The feeling is mutual."

Their lips met in another kiss, one that transcended mere touch. In that embrace, there was a magic far more potent than that held in the hand of a legend. It was a magic born from the depths of sweet, sweet love.

About Janet Koops

A former librarian, Janet is a happily married empty-nester who writes full-time from her home just east of the Rocky Mountains. Explore Janet's literary world further by visiting her official website. There, you'll find a comprehensive list of her published works. Additionally, become a part of Janet's reading community by subscribing to her newsletter, where you'll receive updates, insights, and exclusive content directly from the author.

Scan the QR code
or visit https://janetkoops.com